A STATEN ISLAND LOVE LETTER 5

THE FORGOTTEN BOROUGH

JAHQUEL J.

TEXT UCP TO 22828 TO SUBSCRIBE TO OUR MAILING LIST
If you would like to join our team, submit the first 3-4 chapters of your completed manuscript to Submissions@UrbanChapterspublications.com

This book is dedicated to all the children who were bullied and felt you had no other choice, but to end your life. We love you. We pray for you. And we're here for you.
To those that are victims of bullying, it gets better. There is sun at the end of the tunnel. We're here for you!

-Jahquel J.

Note From The Author:

The finale. Seriously. Enjoy, and if you have a complaint, I told yo' ass not to read it if you were gonna complain. This for my readers who asked for it. Period.

Bless up,
Jah!
The Playlist To This Series --- Listen Here!

Make sure to follow me on social media!
www.facebook.com/JahquelJ
http://www.instagram.com/_Jahquel
http://www.twitter.com/Author_Jahquel
Be sure to join my reader's group on Facebook
www.facebook.com/ Jahquel's we reading or nah?
ANSWER THE QUESTIONS, PLEASE!

1

Staten

"Mami, what the fuck are you doing?" Maliah screamed as the bullet grazed my shoulder. If I hadn't moved when I did, that shit would have hit me right in the chest.

After being shot up more than a few times a while back, I was grateful that this shit grazed my shoulder. Maliah stomped down the stairs and went straight up to her mother and father. Rasheed had snatched the gun out of Messiah's hand and was staring at her just as confused as the rest of us. Messiah had a nonchalant expression on her face like she hadn't just tried to end my life in the middle of broad daylight. Neighbors were filing out of their houses, so Rasheed tossed the gun inside of her opened car door.

"Did you hear those gunshots?" Maliah's neighbor asked, as she eyed down Messiah and Rasheed.

I could tell from Maliah's expression she didn't know what to say. How could she deny seeing it when I was standing here with a bloody shoulder? "My boyfriend's gun had fell off his holster and accidentally went off. We're sorry if it interrupted you," she lied.

"I'm sorry. I thought my holster was secured and the safety on my gun was on," I added on to her lie.

"Is it legal?"

"Of course," I leaned in closer. "I'm a DEA agent, so I would appreciate if this didn't get back to them. One harmless accident and they'll be ready to sit me behind a desk," I chuckled.

I could tell from her expression that she was believing everything that I had said. "They're so hard on their workers, but not enough on these street hooligans," she sucked her teeth. "Your secret is safe with me... thank you for letting me know," she smiled and tapped Maliah's shoulder.

We all watched as she told the rest of the neighbors the bullshit excuse and then went back into her house. I shook my head because Messiah was being reckless as fuck with what she pulled. My mind was getting to Liberty and now I had to deal with this shit.

"Get in the house now," Rasheed said through gritted teeth.

Messiah rolled her eyes and walked past us on the stairs and entered the house. Maliah followed behind and I followed behind her, with Rasheed closing and locking the door behind us. I went into the kitchen where Maliah started cleaning out the wound and shit. I wasn't worried about this shit; I was more worried about how shit would pan out between me and Messiah.

"What the fuck was that about?" Rasheed's voice roared through the house. "Do you know how fucking reckless that was? I was going to come by later, but something told me to come soon as I landed, and I find you doing this shit!"

"Maybe if you came home more often then you would know what was going on. Staten is fucking our daughter," she shook her head. Her voice was so low, yet even, that you wouldn't have assumed she was bothered by it.

"You telling me something that I already knew. I may be always on the go, but I know what the fuck goes on in the streets and with my daughters."

"And you didn't think to fucking tell me? This is what I mean by you keeping shit from me!" Messiah raised her voice. "I should be told on what is going on with my daughters."

"Um, I'm a grown woman. Nothing should be discussed about my life. Mami, you need to realize that I'm grown and can make my own decisions. Both me and Mariah are old enough to decide what we want to happen in our lives."

"Staten is like fucking family," she stood up from the couch and looked at me. "And you, I trusted you around my daughter and you took advantage of her."

"Messiah kill all that shit. You know like I know that pussy comes a dime a dozen. Do you really think I would take advantage of her?"

"She's twenty-one. You're in your thirties. What do you want with her? She's young."

"She's young when it comes to dating, but when you got her moving more weight than a fucking cartel it's fine, right?" she was silent and sat back down on the couch. "You tried to fucking kill me before coming to talk to me.... We're family and you couldn't come and talk to me first?"

She remained silent.

"Yo' crazy ass ain't got shit to say now, huh?" Rasheed stood over her with his arms crossed. I could tell he was pissed at what his wife did.

"She's pregnant," Messiah revealed.

Rasheed looked at Maliah. "This true?"

"Yeah. I'm keeping my baby too. I don't want to hear anything about getting rid of my mistake, like Mami said."

"Your body, your choice. Is this what you want though?"

"Yes."

"And you?" he looked at me.

"I know it's my baby and I'm gonna make sure I'm in my child's life. No matter what."

Rasheed sighed and sat down. "I need to get up with you. Alone."

"Tell me the time and the place," I replied.

Me and Maliah wasn't something I had planned. I also couldn't front like I wasn't falling for her. She had always been my little homie or Messiah's crazy ass twin. I never imagined that we would be fucking and having a baby together. The shit was crazy. Still, I would never intentionally hurt her, and I put that on my daughter.

"I can't wait to talk to your brother about this."

"Nah, he doesn't need to know about this right now. He has too much on his plate right now," I told her and plopped down on the couch.

"I'm gonna call the doctor, you need stitches," Maliah grabbed her phone and left out of the living room.

"Like what? Retirement isn't all that glamorous," Rasheed laughed. "I tried that and was bored the first week."

"He has cancer," I hadn't told anyone and I'm sure that Ghost wouldn't want anyone else knowing, but they needed to know.

Messiah leaned up and stared at me. "Are you kidding me?"

"Yeah. He been doing his treatments and trying to be there for Free. She had the baby and he has a heart condition," It was like diarrhea, once the words came out, they wouldn't stop.

"I need to go by there today. Why doesn't he tell me these things?"

"I don't know... you might shoot him with the way you over-act," I cut my eyes at her.

She stood up. "If I wanted to kill you, you know I would never miss. If you would have stayed still, that bullet would have flew past your ear and into the window shutter. You decided to move."

Messiah was right. Her aim was on point, so if she wanted to kill me, no moving on my end would have stopped that. "Still don't matter. You pulled a gun on me and pulled the trigger."

"You pulled your dick out and fucked my daughter... we're even. Maliah, I don't care what your father is saying, get rid of the baby," Messiah said as she headed out the door.

Rasheed walked over to me and dapped me up. "Get up with me this week. I leave for Egypt next week. I'm surprising Messiah for our anniversary."

"Keep her ass over there," I laughed.

"Yeah, don't tempt me," he joked. "Maliah, call me when you get a chance," he called out to her before he was the next one to head out of the door.

Maliah came and sat down soon after they left. "The doctor can be here in an hour. After you can head to the hospital. I gotta make a run to Jersey to check one of the traps," she informed me.

I stared at her as she consumed herself with her phone. "Why you so quiet?"

I'm fucking embarrassed. My parents come in here asking questions like I'm a child. That shit is so fucking annoying," she vented.

"You worried I'm looking at you like a little girl or some shit?"

"No, because I know I'm not. I'm just annoyed that they won't let me live my life. My mother went against my Papi and fell in love with my father. I just want to be able to have a life when I'm done running the streets. I give my twin a lot of shit about what she chose to do, but I admire her too. She wants to have a life."

"I hear you. I'm not looking at you any different either. Your mother is your moms. She does what she wants and doesn't care what anyone has to say. We're good," I grabbed her and pulled her over to my lap.

"You sure?" she asked and looked down into my eyes. "I don't want this to come up later on... you can run now," she chuckled.

"We're good. Promise," I reached up and kissed her on the lips. "Plus, ain't no running now. We're having a baby together, right?"

"Uh huh. I can't lie, I'm nervous as hell about this. I never been somebody's mother. How can I manage this and still handle what needs to be done?"

"What am I here for? Whatever you lack, I'll pick up the slack and get it done. I want you to promise me something right now."

"What's that?"

"That no matter what, you won't jeopardize our child's life for the streets. The moment I see that shit happen, Maliah..." I allowed my voice to trail off. "I want to know that my child's life means something to you; that you'll step away if that means hurting them."

She looked at me and nodded her head. As much as she liked to blame her mother for her childhood, she was her mother's child. They craved and loved the streets. "Promise," she sealed her promise with a kiss.

"Ight. I'm gonna hold you to the shit too," I told her and she giggled.

"Whatever," she got up and went to answer the door for the doctor.

Staten Island University Hospital

The doctor came and stitched me up and was on his way in under an hour. After I changed my clothes, I headed out to the hospital. Priest kept me updated on everything and the closer I got to the room, my heart was beating faster and faster. Why would she go back to fucking around with that shit? She promised me that she would never do it again. My heart broke because this was the reason I wanted to monitor her. She thought I was being overprotective and wanted to act like her father, but that wasn't the truth. I wanted to make sure she didn't fuck her life up like she did before. Liberty had more to lose than she thought. As much as her aunt raised Chance, he still needed her more than she knew. I tried to be everything for her, and clearly I wasn't enough or I was too much. I rounded the corner and saw Freedom and Justice standing outside of her room talking. When they saw me, they rushed over to me and hugged me.

"Did you know she was back using? Is that why you guys broke up?" Free was the first to ask.

I finished hugging them and shook my head. "Nah, she wanted space and ended things. I didn't think she was back on that shit. If I would have known, I definitely wouldn't have given her the space she asked for."

"How did we all miss this?" Justice sighed. The stress was all over her face. It wasn't too long ago she had her baby, and then had Priest's dumb ass show up after fucking his ex-girlfriend all damn day. I could tell Sis was tired and now she was dealing with her sister overdosing.

"What exactly happened?" I asked Justice.

She sighed and leaned on the wall. "I was leaving to go see my baby. When I got to her truck, I realized I didn't have the keys for it. I went back upstairs and looked on my own for it, because I thought she was asleep. When I went to wake her and she didn't wake up, I knew something was wrong, so I called the ambulance and they came quickly. When they lifted her, there were three baggies with white residue," she wiped away her tears.

"She needs to go back to rehab," Freedom comforted Justice

and stared at me. "A month isn't going to cut it; she needs to get the help that she needs."

"I agree with you. She's not going to take that coming from me, but I'll support the decision and put the money up for it."

"I can pay," Freedom insisted.

"Nah, I want to," I told her.

Justice broke down crying. "I'm just so tired of all of this happening. I'm so damn tired that I can't even sleep at night. I sit and cry anytime I have a moment to myself. First Yasmine, then Priest and now this, how much more can I take?"

"Ma, none of this is your fault so you need to know that we don't blame you. This is happening to all of us... Yasmine's my niece too, and Priest is a dick head. Trust you gonna get through this shit, I promise."

"I don't even want to stay in the apartment anymore. I'm gonna always look at her couch and envision her laid out unconscious." Each time she wiped her tears away, more came down her cheeks.

"You can stay with us." Free offered.

"You live all the way in Jersey. I need to be close to my baby."

"Stay with me. I have a guest suite that you can use. I'm on Staten Island and when baby girl comes home, you can still stay. It's just me and I'm not there most nights anyway."

"Really, Staten?"

"Yeah, I got all that house for no reason."

She hugged me tightly. "I really appreciate it. I really do."

"Don't mention it. You family, I got you," I kissed her on the forehead. "What are they saying?"

"They gave her some medication to help reverse what she took. The doctor said that it was a good thing that Justice noticed her when she did. If she would have been left.... She wouldn't have survived," Freedom informed me.

"Damn. This better open her eyes up to who she is hurting," I sighed.

Liberty was being selfish. I understood she battled things that she chose not to speak on, but what she was doing was fucking selfish. She had all these people that cared for and loved her, yet she still felt the need to go and do that shit. Her son should have been the top of her list of people that needed her, but she continued to go and get high. I'm tired of loving and wanting the best for her, more than she wanted for her own self. That shit was tiring, and I was tired of fighting somebody to love their life and want better for themselves.

"She awake?"

"No. The doctor gave her some stuff that would keep her asleep. Once they were able to get her up, she was fighting with them, so they sedated her," Justice replied.

"How long you both been here?"

"Since Justice called me this morning," I looked at my watch and it was around six in the evening. Both of them had babies they needed to get home to.

"Go see Yasmine, take my car," I handed Justice the keys to my whip. "You head home and be with Ghost and the kids, they need you. I'll sit here with her and see you both tomorrow," I told them.

I could tell the both of them wanted to protest, but knew I was right. They had been up here for hours and needed to go and relax. Sitting up here while she slept wasn't going to do them any good, and they both knew it.

"Okay," Free finally agreed. "I'll be up here tomorrow morning."

"Nah, you will be up there with Ghost while he gets treatment, then you'll go and see Samoor because he gets out of the NICU soon. I'll update you when something changes. I love Liberty, but your sister did this to herself and you and Justice can't keep putting shit off in your lives because she keeps relapsing."

"She's my sister, Staten," Free's voice shook as she said the words. I could tell she wanted to break down and cry.

"Yeah, and she knew what the fuck was going on in your life when she went and got high. Call it for what it is. As much as you care for her, you can't abandon your family that needs you."

Freedom wanted to curse me out and tell me I was wrong, yet she knew that I was right. Liberty knew what was going on in both her sister's lives. She still decided to go and get high. Freedom couldn't drop her life because her twin chose to continue getting high. She had kids that needed her, a new baby with a heart condition and a man battling cancer. As much as she wanted to be here for her sister, she needed to go home and be with her family. Liberty was grown when she made the decision to get high and now she had to be grown and face the consequences of getting high.

"He's right, Free. As much as we want to be here, I need to go and be with my baby. I love Liberty, but how much more can we take? What if she didn't survive? We would have been having to plan a funeral on top of all the shit we have going on. I'll be up here tomorrow, but I'm going to spend time with my daughter. Thank you again, Staten," she hugged me and her sister before she headed down the hallway.

Free looked up at me with tears in her eyes. "I can't lose her, Staten. My life feels like I'm in a bad dream. Between her and Gyson, I can't lose either of them."

I hugged her tightly because I felt the same way about the both of them. My brother was my rock, the man I looked up to and seeing him so weak and battling cancer had me in a fucked-up state. Then, Liberty was the love of my life and she was still using drugs and overdosed. My mind wasn't in the right place either.

"We'll make sure this time she won't relapse. Go home and get some rest... ight?" she nodded her head and put her purse on her arm. "Call me when you make it home."

"I will," she replied as she pulled herself together.

After Justice and Freedom left, I went into Liberty's room and looked at her. She looked so angelic laying in the bed. Her hair was up in a bun that was once neat, but with all that had gone on, it was now pieces lying in her face. I sat down beside her bed and pulled my phone out and sent Maliah a message.

Here... prob gonna stay for the night. You good?

Yeah, I'm heading to grab some food and then going home. Today has been a day, she replied.

Word. You good tho, right?

Yes, Staten lol. I'm ok. Be there for Lib. Tell her that I'm wishing her well.

Bet.

I put my phone on the table beside the bed and laid my head back and closed my eyes. Disappointment was an understatement for what I felt. I was so mad that she slipped back into her old ways. Part of me felt like it was my fault. I allowed her to push me away and stopped checking up on her. Even with us breaking up, I should have done my part as her friend and been there for her. Instead, I was too angry and hurt to even reach out to her. If we were still together none of this would have happened. I folded my arms and laid back in the chair to get some sleep and hope she woke up soon.

2

Justice

I know they said God didn't give you too much, but I felt like he was tossing buckets of water on me and expecting me to stay dry. Everything was falling apart in my world and I didn't know what to do. I didn't have any more tears left to cry, so I sucked it up and wore a somber expression on my face. Visiting my baby girl was the highlight of my day and I couldn't bring myself to smile or laugh at her little expressions. *What did I do that was so horrible? Why did I deserve this?* All I tried to do is be a good person and help people, yet I get fucked over in the end. I was tired of being good to everyone and then I was the one who got the short end of the stick.

When I walked into Liberty's apartment and found her unresponsive, I thought my sister was dead. My first actions were to sit there and cry, but another side of me emerged and I did CPR while on the phone with EMS. I thought Liberty had gotten clean and was working toward bettering her relationship with Chance. This entire time she made us think that she was getting clean and she wasn't. I felt bad as fuck because I didn't notice the signs. As her sister I should have noticed that she wasn't herself and was back using. I agreed with what Staten said; she knew what she did before she did it. As much as I loved my sister, I had to focus my time and energy on my baby girl. She was my main priority right now. With everything going on between me and Priest, I needed to focus on her and give her my all.

I rocked in the chair as I watched her moving slowly around in the incubator. The feeding tube attached to the side of her face and then going up her nose, always pissed me off. As a parent, you never wanted to see your child going through this. I would have rather have my ass laying in a hospital bed than to have her struggle to breathe. I felt like I failed as a parent by having her early. I heard the NICU door open and looked at Priest coming in. He was drying his hands off and then tossed the paper towels into the bin. I've become the expert at avoiding him. I asked the nurses what time he came and tried to come hours before he did. Once, I almost bumped into him, but he was in a heated argument on the phone, so he didn't notice me turn around and go the other direction.

"What's up?" he sat in the empty chair next to Yasmine's incubator.

"Hey," I replied dryly. Man, I was so bitter, angry and all of those things that women went through. I hated him. I wanted to slap and hurt him like he had hurt me.

I started gathering my stuff to leave and he touched my arm. "You don't have to leave when I come."

I gently took my arm back. "I'd rather go. Thanks though," I tossed out the food I was eating.

I had been up here since I left the hospital with Staten and Freedom. The hours were twenty-four hours for parents. All the nurses loved me so they would give me blankets and bring coffee for me in the morning. I needed to go and bring Staten his car back and see if he could help me move my clothes out of Liberty's apartment.

"Can we talk real quick?"

"No thanks."

"Justice, can we talk? We haven't talked at all."

"For wh... meet me in the hall," I had raised my voice and I had to remember that there were other parents and babies in here.

I said goodbye to the nurses and then stood down the hall waiting for Priest to show his ass up. When I was two minutes from leaving, he finally came into the hall. "Look, Jus... there's nothing I can say th—"

"You're right. There is nothing you can say that would make this better. You missed our daughter being born because you were fucking your ex. Might I add, an ex that you told me not to worry about. You were one of the good ones, Priest," I shook my head. "You made me think you were one of the good ones, I let my guard down with you."

"Baby, I fucke—"

"I trusted you and you fucked me over like my ex. All I wanted was what we had."

"Ma, I want to make this work with you and fix everything. If I gotta jump through hoops, then that's what I have to do."

"Whatever. Go jump through hoops for that bitch that was more important than your daughter," I turned to walk down the hall.

"Don't do that, ma."

"Nigga, I didn't do shit, you did. Spend time with your daughter," I replied and pressed the button for the elevator.

Priest had wasted enough time of mine and I wasn't about to waste another second on his mess. He wanted to be sorry because his ass got caught. If I never saw the evidence on him, he would have continued to have his cake and eat it too. I had bigger things to worry about other than him and his guilt. If you asked me, I hoped that shit ate him alive at night. I appreciated Staten for offering his home, but I needed to get it on my own. I had left one relationship and ended up depending on Priest more than I should have. I needed my own independence. It was time for me to make a home for me and my daughter.

After I left the hospital, I met with Staten at Staten Island hospital. If I never seen another hospital I would have been satisfied. He was waiting downstairs when I pulled up. He got into the car and then put his head back.

"Why the fuck is life so hard?" he randomly asked with his eyes still closed. "I feel like I'm trying to swim, but these damn waves keep taking me out," I knew he had a lot on his plate.

"I feel the same way. Look at it like this, we're strong and we're going to keep swimming. It's hard, but it will get better."

"You right."

"I know. I have to be right, cause I can't take anymore."

"I feel you. Liberty is still not up. The doctors checked her vitals and she's good but hasn't woke up yet."

"Damn."

"I hope she's well rested for what the fuck I'm about to say to her when she wakes up."

I pulled off from the front of the hospital and headed toward his house. "Do you still love her?"

"Yeah. Liberty got my heart. I don't know if she knows or believes me, but I love her ass more than myself sometimes."

You haven't been by to see the baby at all. Tf! A Text message popped up on the dashboard screen. When he entered the car, his phone automatically connected to the Bluetooth in the car.

"Then I gotta deal with shit like this," he sighed.

"How is Satin?"

"Good. She look so much like her damn mother. I pray she don't act like her either," he lightly joked.

"One day at a time."

"Huh?"

"Take everything one day at a time. The world wasn't built in a day, so you shouldn't expect to fix everything in one. Go spend some time with your daughter. Not because Chanel is bitching about it, but because you need to feel the warmth that a baby gives you. I'm on cloud nine after seeing my baby."

"How is Yasmine?"

"She's doing better. Still has the feeding tube and she's still struggling to keep her body heat outside of the incubator, so she's still in there."

"Damn, I gotta come up to see her."

"You can come anytime you want. But, spend time with Satin."

He nodded his head. "When you want to move in?"

"About that?" I giggled.

"What now?"

"I appreciate your offer and I'm gonna stay for a week or so, but I'm gonna get my own place. I've been saving up money that Priest gives me and I'm gonna get me an apartment."

"Word. Why?"

"I need to learn independence again. Priest covered everything. I didn't have to pay or lift a finger and I became comfortable."

"I wouldn't say you didn't lift a finger. You had those girls in check."

"True, but I didn't have to. I got so comfortable with him covering everything and that wasn't okay. He even covered the unexpected expenses for my center when he didn't have to. I got so comfortable and I'm ready to provide for myself. Staten, I was a damn teacher with my own car, and apartment. I've allowed men to break me down 'til I couldn't function, and I refuse to allow this to happen with Yasmine depending on me."

"Yass sis, period pooh. Ain't that what y'all say?"

I busted out laughing. "I so needed that laugh right now."

"Priest is a dumb ass and neither me or Ghost support what the fuck what he did. That shit was wrong and I'm not gonna lie because he's my brother. He did that shit for a bitch that was his past."

"Yeah, it sucks because I love that man so much."

"I could tell. He loves you too, but let shit side-track him. Do you think you both can come back from this?"

I sighed and bit on my bottom lip. "Right now... no."

"I respect it."

"I just need to get my life back on track and focus on my child. He doesn't matter right now. Yasmine has my full attention and if Priest can't understand that, then maybe this was a blessing in disguise."

And you ignoring me! Probably with that bitch Liberty!!!!!!!! Another message popped up on his car's screen.

"She always concerned with who I'm with like we're together."

"This is why you don't fuck your friends, Staten. That should have never been a line crossed, especially with all the money you have. You should have just jerked off in a cup and had that shit injected into her. Chanel gone off the dick and now she has your child so she about to milk it."

"Yeah, I've been told a time or two."

We need to talk about baby #2. I want Satin to have a sister or brother close in age. She sent another message and I gulped.

"She serious?"

"When she can't get a hold of me, she sends something dramatic to get me to respond. I don't know how many times she told me she thought she was in labor to get me to stop by her crib or answer her calls."

"You both are in this together and the main goal is to raise that baby together. She needs to cut the dramatics and you need to be there more so she doesn't have an excuse to use that you're absent. If you have to bring the baby to your house for the weekend, do it."

"You would let Priest bring Yasmine to his crib once she's home?"

"Yep. As much as I hate him right now, he's an amazing uncle to the girls and I know he'll be an amazing father to Yasmine. If he could raise three girls alone, I have all the trust that she'll be fine for a day or two."

"Justice, you dope man. You have so many reasons and excuses to hate this man and put dirt on his name, but you still find a way to compliment him."

"I do hate him," I smirked. "I refuse to let our personal issues get in the way of parenting our child. In the end, she didn't have anything to do with our issues, so why punish her with a bad co-parenting relationship... you know?"

"Yeah, I feel you. You know where you want to move yet?"

"Well, I'm on a budget, so I'm thinking about moving back to my old apartment building. My old apartment isn't available, the one on the lower floor is."

"For real? You don't think it's too many bad memories."

"In that old apartment, yeah. But, I'm so ready to make new memories and make us a home. I have a meeting to go speak with my old land lord and put a deposit down on the apartment."

"You move fast as shit."

"Yeah, well I had a bunch of time sitting in the NICU last night, so I was researching things. I know I won't be able to move in until the beginning of the month, so that's where you'll come in," I laughed.

"You're free to stay there. I don't have an issue with that."

"Thanks."

"Where you going?"

"I'm dropping you off to Chanel's parents' house. I know she's there and you need to spend time with your baby girl."

"Bruh, how you just gonna force me?"

"Despite how Chanel makes you feel, you have to ignore that because your daughter is the most important."

We pulled up to Chanel's parents' house and Staten sighed. "Appreciate the talk, Justice."

"Anytime. I'm gonna go back to Liberty's house and grab my clothes," I informed him. "I'm gonna stop by Priest's house and get some more clothes while he's visiting Yasmine," he handed me the key to his house.

"You know the address... pick any room, just not mine."

"I got you," I laughed. "And thanks for letting me use your car to get around."

"You're good. I'll have one of my youngins' come and pick me up. Drive safe." Chanel's parents must have had cameras because she opened the front door and was standing there with her hand on her hips.

"Make it a peaceful visit."

"It's never peaceful when her parents are around," he shrugged his shoulders and closed the door. He walked around the back of the car, tapped the trunk and I pulled off.

I SPENT the past few days moving clothes and anything I had into Staten's house. Priest wasn't happy that I kept coming when he wasn't there. He wanted to sit down and talk, and that was the last thing I wanted to do. I was hurt, angry and bitter. That bitch came into our lives for a matter of a few weeks and she was able to take what was mine. Priest was mine. I made him whole again after being broken for so many years. She was able to take something and share something that I thought was only reserved for me and him. It hurt me to think that he had sex with her and enjoyed it. As much as he wanted to fix things, I wasn't in the mood to fix anything. In my eyes, he had done the worst thing he could have possibly done to me. If the cheating wasn't bad enough, he was so consumed with his cheating that he missed the birth of our daughter. Tears always came to my eyes when I thought about how I would reminisce on the birth of my daughter, and his cheating and missing her birth would always be in the back of my head. Of course, I would never tell her what happened between me and her father, but I would know and that was just as bad.

"Sorry, I'm late. Zamari was cutting up with Love before I left," Kiss came to the table and hugged me.

She wanted to meet at a coffee shop to talk. I sipped my coffee and looked at her as she placed her Givenchy Antigona purse on the empty chair. Kiss loved to shop with her uncle's money. That bag cost over two thousand dollars, and here she was a new mother rocking that bag. Some mothers couldn't afford a Michael Kors bag and she was walking around carefree with this bag. That was the perk of living with Priest. He was generous with money and it was nice to be able to shop whenever you want, but I refused to stay with a man because of what he could offer.

"How's my baby boo doing?"

"Bad as hell," she rolled her eyes. "With you gone, I've had to step in with him and the girls," she sighed.

"Well, do you see how hard it was for me?"

"Absolutely. I wanted to talk to you about some things that have been on my chest."

"Okay..."

"I want to thank you for everything you've done for me. I know I've been so ungrateful and a down right bitch about everything. Even with me acting like that, you've always been there for me and never turned your back on me, and I appreciate it."

"Kiss, you know I would do anything for you and the girls. I love you, Zamari and the girls so much."

"I know you do. My mom died when I was young, so it's

hard for me to trust women. Especially when my uncle is involved. Women only want to be bothered with us because of him and his money. He always makes sure to let them know we're a package deal, and they agree, but then they realize that his life isn't as glamorous and carefree like they originally thought. Marisol and his relationship were on the low, so we didn't know until it was ending and she wasn't working with us anymore. When you came in, I was hesitant because of your situation. But, the more you were around, the more I saw how much you cared for me and the girls. I just wanted to apologize for all that I've been doing and how I've been acting."

I reached across the table and touched her hand. "I'll always be there for you girls. It doesn't matter if me and your uncle are together or not."

"I know that now," she took a break. "I'm pregnant again," she revealed.

I dropped my head because I knew this would happen. Reese was a good man and he cared and took care of both she and Zamari, even with Zamari not being his, but I knew that she would end up pregnant again.

"Jus, please don't look like that," she whined.

"I'm disappointed, Kiss. You're supposed to be in college and doing something, what are you going to do with two babies?"

"I was thinking about getting an abortion without telling Reese. He would be pissed because he wants to have a baby of his own."

"Reese can take care of it, but it's more than that. What about you and your life? You can't just float around on your uncle and Reese's money. You need something for you. A degree and a career."

I could tell that she wasn't trying to hear anything I was saying. In her eyes, she had landed another big fish and wanted to have this baby because of Reese. Reese's status in the streets had grown and he was now one of Staten's main go to men. More money was coming in and his status was rising in the streets. Still, that didn't mean that Kiss needed to go and get pregnant by him. Zamari was not even a year yet and she was already pregnant with baby number two.

"I wasn't trying to get pregnant, but I'm not going to get an abortion if my man wants the baby. I know and I've been thinking about going to take some college classes to pass time."

"Pass time? What do you mean pass time? You need to take college classes to get a degree. Kiss, no man wants a woman that isn't about nothing. Trust me, I've had the career and everything and now look at me."

"What do you mean look at you? You have a center about to open up and you're an incredible teacher, Justice. Stop being so hard on yourself, you're goals."

I laughed. "Girl, I'm not goals. Having a baby by Priest is not goals. Although, some chicks in the hood might beg to differ."

"I'm saying you're goals because you got a man that couldn't care less if a female fucked with him or not, in the house going crazy. Ro loves the shit out of you. I'm not defending his recent actions, but I know that he really does love you."

"Yeah, I believed that once upon a time ago," I rolled my eyes. "Did you tell him about the baby?"

"No. I have to tell Reese first. We've been talking about buying a house together." Kiss was delusional about her happily ever after with Reese.

"A house?"

"Yeah, his house is nice, but too small for me, Zamari and the new baby. Plus, he wants to rent that out. He was talking about a bigger house out in Tottenville."

"Did he say he wanted you to move in?"

"No, but I'm about to have his baby so I know he'll move me in there."

"Kiss, how about you get your own apartment? It's nothing

like getting your own for you and Zamari. Move from your uncle's house to your own shit, not another man."

Even though she looked me right in the eye and was listening to everything that I said, she was going to do what she wanted to do. In her mind, moving into a bigger home with Reese with her son and their baby was goals to her. Yeah, she'd be the talk of the hood for a while because a lot of people wanted to land Reese, but then what? What happened when he was gone for the day or days working in the trap and she had two kids to take care of? Reese already felt like she didn't need a nanny or shouldn't have been partying and leaving me to watch the baby. So, with her under his roof, he wasn't about to put up with partying and pawning the kids off on anybody.

"Justice, I don't want to be judged. I'm trying to do what is best for me and Zamari. Moving in with Reese is what is best and what I want to do."

"Okay, I support you. If you need anything you let me know... okay?"

"I will," she smiled at me. "Now, how is my beautiful baby cousin?"

"She's good. I'm heading there now to go and see her. I'm hoping she'll be able to come home soon."

"Me too. She's gonna be so spoiled. I already have stuff in my room that I had bought for her."

"She has enough stuff over at the house, you need to stop buying her stuff. I have to go and get some stuff for her room at my new place."

"New place? You move quick."

"Yeah. I'm tired of bouncing from house to house. I like having my own space and with a baby, I *need* my own place."

"I hear you. I'm glad that you're in a good place, seriously. I was worried about you."

I giggled. "I should be worried about you, not the other way around. How's the girls?"

"Love is messing around with some twenty-year-old in Stapleton. Priest doesn't know and I confronted her on it, and she refuses to stop messing with him."

"Twenty-year-old? She's sixteen years old, Kiss. Have you told Priest?"

"No, I'm handling it before getting him involved. She's not having sex, thank God."

"How do you know? You lied about being pregnant for a full pregnancy... I need to go and talk with Love."

"Don't tell her I told you anything. I found out who the nigga is and I'm gonna go and talk to him and let him know. I'm sure Love didn't tell him how old she really is."

"You girls are going to be the death of me? What about Kiki?"

"She's good. Having little friend issues, they picking on her and shit. You know regular middle school stuff."

"Don't take that too lightly. Make sure you check on your sister and see if she's alright," I told her.

Bullying wasn't like it was when I was growing up. We would call each other names and then that was it. Now, bullying happened at school and because of social media, it followed them home. It wasn't something to take lightly and I was going to make sure I checked on Kiki. I also needed to talk with Priest so he could make sure he was checking in with her as well. With all we had going on, it was easy for the girls to get lost in the shuffle of our chaos.

We sat and ordered some pastries and continued to catch up on each other's lives. Kiss was a good kid; she was just misguided and didn't have a woman to teach her the way to be a woman. Her uncle tried his best, but he wasn't a woman and it was hard to try and raise a girl into a woman being a man. I wouldn't say that he didn't do a good job, because he did. He did the best he could with what he had and that counted for something. At the end of the day, Kiss was spoiled, bratty and wanted things to be done on her terms. She wanted little to no advice and as a man, you didn't know how to deal with that. Kiss wanted to meet to tell me what she was gonna do, not seek advice. Although I always inserted my own advice, she ultimately did what she wanted in the end. I finished up with Kiss and promised to invite the girls over for movie night at Staten's house this weekend. I missed them so much and this weekend would be like old times. Staten didn't lie when he said he was barely home. I had been using his car like it was mine and he didn't mind. He had others that he drove so I could use this one. I jumped into the car, started it and headed to see my angel at the hospital.

3

Freedom

I rocked in the glider in Samoor's nursery as I watched him sleep peacefully in his crib. Since he got home, I couldn't sleep a full night. Nights like this, I would warm me up some milk in my favorite mug and sit in his nursery while watching him. To me, he was the most fragile out of all our children and the one I would forever worry about. His heart couldn't take too much so I wanted to take all his stress away. I rocked as I looked at his perfect heart shaped lips, bushy eyebrows like Samaj and Ghost, and a dimple in one of his cheeks like his smallest sister. He was so perfect to me. Perfection almost always came in the storm of imperfection. Right now, our home was in an uproar of chaos and I was doing my best to float through it and be there for everyone. Ghost's treatments were making him weaker by the day. He could no longer hide it from the kids anymore, but he refused to tell them. His fear was that it would scare them, and he didn't want them to have to worry.

"Couldn't sleep again?" I looked toward the door and Samaj was standing at the door. He had a glass of water in his hands.

"Nope," I smiled. "Don't grow up, you'll have this thing called worry," I made a light joke. He walked into the room and sat on the floor in front of me.

"Is Pops alright?" Out of both of the twins, Samaj was very self-aware. I could never hide anything from him. Even when I thought he wasn't watching; he was and would always prove that I wasn't as sly as I thought I was.

"He's fine, baby," I lied.

"Ma, you told us that lying is bad."

"I'm not lying."

"You're a terrible liar just like Somali. You both can't lie to save your life," he called me out.

"Baby, I think daddy should be the one to tell you."

"Tell him what?" Ghost's voice sounded in the room. You could tell from his frame that he was losing weight. He barely had an appetite and when he did eat something, he would throw it up soon after.

"Are you alright?" Samaj directed his question to his father.

"Yeah, I'm good... don't worry about me." Ghost tried to end the subject, but his headstrong son wasn't having it. "Why you looking at me like that?" Ghost asked Samaj.

"Because the both of you are lying to me. I'm eleven now, you can tell me stuff," he tried to convince us.

Ghost walked into the nursery and pulled me up from the glider and sat down. He pulled me onto his lap as we looked at our son. "Tell him, Ma," heave me permission to tell Samaj.

"Daddy has cancer," my voice cracked. I had said it in my head so many times, but it was something about saying it out loud that made it real for me.

"Are you going to die?"

"Maj, you think I'm a punk?"

"No, you're the strongest man I know," he smiled at his father.

"So, just know that I'm beating cancer's ass, ight?"

"Okay."

"Give me and your mother a hug and go back to bed," he told him and he got up to hug the both of us.

"Pops?"

"Yeah."

"Make sure you beat cancer. It would suck to lose you after just getting you," he said and the tears fell down my face.

"I got you," he nodded at him.

When Samaj left the room, Ghost hugged me tightly as I sobbed hard. "I can't lose you again, Gyson."

"You're not, babe. Stop all this crying. I'm doing what needs to be done and I got this," he tried to convince me.

I was so scared and worried all the time. I couldn't do this life without him. Me and the kids needed him. "I love you so much."

"And I love you too. I need you to do something for me."

"Anything," I turned and looked into his face.

"We need to go to the lawyer's office and sign guardianship papers. If something was to ever happen to me, I want to know that Rain stays with you and you'll raise her right."

"Don't talk like that."

"Ma, I have to. It's not even about the cancer. Anything could happen and I want to make sure my daughter is straight."

"What about your mother or Mirror?"

"I love my sister and mother, but I want my daughter to be raised with her siblings. She lost her sister and mother, god forbid she loses me too, I need to know that she'll have her siblings to turn to."

He wiped the tears that continued to fall from my eyes and looked me in the eyes. "I'll sign the papers."

"Thank you," he kissed me on the lips. "Let's go to bed before we wake the baby. You got me?"

"Always."

"That's all I need to go to war with cancer," he winked at me and held my hand as we left the baby's room.

When we laid in the bed holding each other in our home that we shared with our children, I couldn't help but to think of doing this alone. None of this shit mattered if Gyson wasn't here to share it with me. I worried all the time about him and how his condition could change. The chemo had already started to mess with him. He was losing weight because he never wanted to eat, and he became nauseous at the drop of a dime. His gums were always hurting and some days it just hurt to move. The chemo did worse than the damn cancer if you asked me. Still, he refused for anybody to help him. He wanted to help himself and didn't want to be looked at as weak. So even when it pained him to walk, he still played with Rain and put her on his back, although it hurt. When he was too tired to keep his eyes opened, he still watched Somali rehearse her dance routine in front of him. Samaj loved to play basketball, so Gyson made sure he was out there to play one on one with him every night before bed.

I smiled on the inside, but on the outside, I worried he was overextending himself. He loved his kids and would always be there for them. He would rather us be happy than worry about his health. It was one of the things that I loved about him, but also one of the things that always made me worry about him too. I laid in his arms and a single tear fell from my eyes.

The entire night, I didn't sleep at all. All I did was toss and turn and think about our life. Ghost left me in bed to sleep while handling the kids before he went to chemo. I tried to come with him, but he told me get some rest and then go and see my sister. Since everything that happened with Ghost and with Samoor having his heart condition, we hired a nanny that came to the house and helped with the children. We even brought her to the hospital to learn more about Samoor if something was to ever happen when she was caring for him.

"Free, you need to pump some more breast milk for Samoor," Ms. Winnie, the nanny popped her head into our bedroom.

I loved Ms. Winnie because she did her job, allowed me to vent when I was having a bad day and she loved our children. The kids loved her too. When we were looking for one, I wanted someone older who was reliable and that I could trust. Work had taken a back seat when it came to everything. My assistant took the lead over my company and I was happy that I could depend on her to do what was needed. My mind had been on Gyson and our son. I didn't have time to put it into my company, and I honestly wasn't in the mood to put my all into designing someone's dream home. I was worried about trying to keep my man alive and making sure my baby made it to see his sixteenth birthday. Then, I had to worry about our other kids and making sure they didn't feel neglected through all of this. Everything was too much, and I felt like I was spiraling down a hill.

"I'll pump some before I head to see Gyson's mother," I told her and rolled back over. Life seemed so unfair and pulling myself out of bed proved to be harder and harder each day.

"Aht, aht," Ms. Winnie said and walked further into my bedroom. She walked over to the window and opened them up. "You don't need to let this pull you into a dark space. You're going through something right now, but guess what? It can't rain forever, baby. The sun will come out and it will make those cloudy and rainy days all worth it."

"It's hard to see the bigger picture when shit keeps happening to me. I'm trying to remain together for everyone, and I feel like I'm coming apart. The kids, Gyson, work and everything else."

"And your mother? She called from her cruise and asked if you were alright. I told her that you would call her back... have you called her?"

I sat up in the bed and shook my head. "My mom isn't good with things like this," I sighed, hoping that it made Ms. Winnie lay off with the questions.

"No one is good with these things. None of that matters when we're all going through things."

Soon as things started to get bad, I informed my mother of everything going on. I cried and told her how I felt, and she comforted me as my mother, yet she didn't cancel her plans to come home and help me out with her grandchildren. I didn't expect her to do it, but at the same time as my mother, I expected that she would want to be there for me.

"Yeah, well my mom is the worst and I don't have the time to be worried about her and everything else that I'm currently dealing with."

"I'll trust you on this one. Pump some milk and get your day started. We won't let the devil win," she smiled and then left out of the room.

"Sure seem like he's winning," I sighed and got up from the bed to start my day.

It took me three hours to pump milk, shower and get dressed. I found myself zoning out during the whole process. It was like I was there and at the same time I wasn't. When it was time to go, I kissed my baby boy and headed toward Mama Rae's house. It had been a while since we sat down and spoke, and she told me that she wanted me to come over today to see her. I didn't have time to sit, drink tea and chat. My life just didn't allow me to do those simple luxuries anymore. However, because it was Mama Rae, I made time to do what she had asked. She had been to the house to help out and took Gyson to chemo when Staten or Priest couldn't. Her small gestures were large when it came to the chaos that I currently lived in on a daily basis.

I killed the engine and got out of the car. Dressed down in jeans, white T-shirt and pair of Valentino sneakers, I strolled to the front door that was always opened. When I opened the door, I could smell the faint smell of blueberry muffins and coffee. Whenever you came through Mama Rae's door, you could always be certain that she was cooking and your nostrils would be met with some kind of tasty aroma that would cause your mouth to water. I hadn't had any appetite lately and my stomach rumbled at the smell of her muffins baking in the oven.

"Where are you, Mama Rae?" I called as I looked through the house. She popped her head out of the laundry room with a smile on her face.

"You're losing too much weight. Have you had anything to eat?" she immediately wondered. Food wasn't big on my list. It was like all the symptoms from Chemo that Ghost was going through, passed through to me. I didn't want to eat and when food was in front of me, I felt nauseous and didn't want to consume anything.

"I'm not worried about the weight that I'm losing. I'm worried about all the weight that Gyson is losing," I reminded her that my focus wasn't on myself.

"How are you going to be great for your family if you're not taking care of yourself? Samoor is a strictly breastfed baby and it takes a lot out of you to produce milk to feed him. How are you going to produce milk if you're not taking care of yourself?"

"I don't know. I'm tired of trying to pretend like I'm fine. And, I'm tired of Gyson acting like he doesn't have cancer and like I'm not supposed to be emotional or feel a certain way."

"Well, you have to understand that he's going through something right now. He may not want to come home from a day at chemo and see his woman upset and crying. It's not that he doesn't care, he just doesn't want to be constantly reminded that he has cancer when he enters his home."

I understood her point and could admit I had been selfish when it came to my feelings and my feelings alone. It usually took someone older to point things out to you for them to make sense.

"I'm going to try and be better about that. Samaj knows about everything."

"Oh yeah? And how did he take that?" she pulled me over to the kitchen and forced me to sit down. I watched her stir something in the pot for a bit before she grabbed a plate, added white rice and spooned some curry goat over my rice.

"He took it well. I can tell he's scared."

"That boy is just like his father. He will hide his fear and work hard to maintain that tough exterior, meanwhile he's breaking down on the inside. Make sure you check in with him and let him know that everything is alright and that you are both there for him," she reminded me. "What about Somali? I know Rain is too young to understand, so I wouldn't tell her right now."

"I don't know when I'm going to tell Somali. She's emotional and doesn't know how to process things without taking it personal."

"Wonder where she gets that from?" Mama Rae laughed.

I tasted the food and took a few spoonful's before I replied back to her. "Well, I can't help that's how I am. I'm trying to be better."

"I heard about Liberty... how's that going?"

Each time someone brought up my twin, I felt like a knife was poked right through my body. I wanted to lie and say everything was alright, but it wasn't. Liberty was sick and needed the right help. People thought that rehab could fix and cure everyone and that was the furthest from the truth. I can't lie and say that I didn't believe that after she was released. To me, Liberty was back to herself and was going to go on the clean and clear path. Then, I had to think about it. She had been doing this drug for years, so it was foolish of me to believe that she would recover in just a month. This was going to be something she fought her entire life, and I had to be there to fight that fight with her. I couldn't wake up to a phone call telling me that my sister was dead. I needed her more than she knew. She had to know that she was loved and there were other ways besides getting high.

"She's still in the hospital. Staten has been up there with her. He told me I needed to focus on Gyson and Samoor."

"He's right," she agreed. "That's your sister, but she has made her bed and now she has to lay in it."

"It's hard to just leave her up there. What if she wakes up and we're not there?"

"Maybe that will make her get her shit together to want to be better. I have a friend and I want you to talk to her daughters."

"Mama Rae, I really don't want to talk to anyone about this."

"Trust me, you'll want to sit and hear what they have to say," she insisted. Only because I was at the end of my rope when it came to Liberty, I was willing to sit down and talk to whoever Mama Rae insisted that I spoke to.

"Okay," I agreed.

"How's the company going?"

"Good. I guess. I haven't paid it much attention since Gyson got sick and since I found out about Samoor's condition."

"Understandable. You need to bring Samoor over here and go get some work done. It will take a lot off your mind. You love to design."

"I can't bring myself to focus on anything that has to do with my company. There is so much going on that it seems like that should be the last thing I should be focused on."

"You can't sit around and wait for the cancer to leave Gyson's body or for Samoor's heart condition to improve. Sitting home waiting for those things to happen will drive you crazy. Go to the office, engross yourself in some work for a few hours and I promise you'll feel better," she tried to convince me.

I didn't know if going into my office was going to improve my mood. Going to work and trying to create beautiful rooms for happy families didn't sound appealing, especially since my own family life was in shambles. For my own mental sake, I would try this because the lord knew I needed something different to happen in my life. We all just needed a small break to catch our breath.

4

Liberty

I'm commitment shy, so when my feelings get involved, I tend to run
– Kevin Gates

I opened my eyes and winced at the sunlight coming through the window. My throat felt like I had sipped on a sand martini and my arms were sore like I had been fighting my way out of a cave filled with spiders. I moved my hands and saw I had an IV stuff into my hand. *What happened?* I thought to myself while trying to piece together what could have happened. Everything kept coming up as a blank. Like, there wasn't one thing that came to mind as to why I was laid up in a hospital room feeling like death. Clearing my throat, I tried to reach for the bottle of water sitting on the table beside my bed. When I realized that I wouldn't be able to reach it, I panicked slightly.

"Thirsty, huh?" an unfamiliar voice asked me. My memory was cloudy, and I couldn't remember how I had ended up here, yet I knew I had never heard that voice before. Was it a nurse, doctor or someone that could hand me this damn bottle of water?"

I nodded my head because it hurt too much to try and talk. Laying in this bed, I couldn't even see who the unfamiliar voice belonged to. I finally stopped trying to get the water and laid my head back onto the bed. Just trying to grab the water was exhausting me. The woman finally came into my view. She was a medium built woman with jet black hair that was pulled into a sleek ponytail. Her toffee colored skin glowed with the sun that came into the room. I watched as she adjusted my bed and I came up in an almost sitting position. She poured some of the water into a Styrofoam cup and placed a plastic straw into the cup. I had never wanted water so bad that I could smell how good that it was. When she put it near my mouth, I grabbed hold of the straw and sucked down the water so fast that I started choking. She patted me on the back while pressing the call button for some help.

The nurse entered the room five seconds later and when she saw me choking, she smiled. I wanted to yell, scream and slap her for laughing at me. Like a child, she had me hold my arms up and patted me on the back a few times before I finally stopped.

"Let me guess... you drank your water down too fast?" she smirked. "Take small sips until you can tolerate more. You've been getting all your hydration through your IV, so your throat has gotten quite used to you not having anything orally," she explained. "I'm glad that you're awake and not fighting. Let me call the PCA in here so she can check your vitals. I'll also page your doctor to let him know that you're up and awake," she told me.

Fighting? What does she mean by I'm not fighting? I was so confused. *Was that the reason that my arms felt like I had been fighting all my life?* The PCA came in almost instantly and took all my vitals while I looked at the woman standing in the corner. *Who was she? Why was she here? Where was my family?* There were so many questions that I needed to ask, yet it hurt to speak. Clearing my throat, I looked at my PCA as she wrapped up the blood pressure cuff up on the small cart she rolled in here with.

"Where's my family?" I whispered.

She looked up from the cart and placed the thermometer into my mouth. "I just came on shift an hour ago, I can go find out and let you know," she told me as she pulled the thermometer out of my mouth. "Your vitals are all good."

"Thank you," I mustered. It hurt like hell to speak.

"No need to find out where her family is. They'll be here soon," the woman spoke. *Who the fuck was she?* She didn't know me from a hole in the wall, so why did she think she could speak for me?

"Oh okay. Well, I'll be back to check your vitals in a couple hours. Lunch is coming up so I'll bring you a tray after speaking to your doctor." And with that, she left me alone with this woman.

"My name is Evelyn," she introduced herself. "I'm good friends with Rae."

Mama Rae was the one who sent this woman. *What was her purpose of sending her?* I wondered to myself. "Liberty."

"Don't strain your voice. Rae asked me to come and speak to you and that's why I'm here. For any moment, you don't want me here, I'm still gonna stay."

"Have no choice, I guess," I mumbled and leaned back onto the bed.

She took a seat on the chair and crossed her legs. "Do you know why you're here?"

I shook my head no.

"You overdosed and your sister found you," she revealed and I gasped. I thought she was going to tell me that I passed out or something. "She found you at the right time because you could have died if she didn't."

"Which sister?"

"Justice."

My heart broke because Justice didn't need any more on her plate. Then, for her to be the one to find me hurt like hell. She was the main one rooting for me to remain clean. I felt like I disappointed a lot of people.

"How long have you been using? I don't mean since you've gotten cleaned, but in total?"

Shit, no one had asked me that. It had been years since I've been getting high. I didn't exactly count and hold anniversary parties each time a year passed by. "Years."

"You knew when you got out of rehab that you would go back, didn't you?" Part of me felt like I knew I would end up back using drugs. Then, the other part of me knew I had to try and be sober. I had Staten, my sisters and Chance counting on me.

"I wanted to be clean for my boyfriend at the time, sister and son," I admitted. My mind told me that I had to be clean for them. There was no other option, other than to be clean.

"You can't be clean for anyone, but yourself. While you're trying to be clean and impress everyone, you're the only person who is suffering. Your family were content because they thought you were clean, meanwhile you were dying on the inside."

Why did this woman know exactly how I was feeling? She hit the nail on the head. I was trying so hard to please everyone and I felt like I was the one losing myself more and more. Shit became hard and I didn't have coke to keep me balanced. The real shit happening to me, I had to handle alone and without the comfort of being high.

"I tried..."

"Trying isn't good enough. It's not good enough when the

people who love you want better for you. Trying only gets you clean long enough to fool your family." Tears fell down my cheeks. She gently touched my arm. "Baby, I can see the pain and hurt you've had to endure alone. You're not alone, I see it."

I knew my family loved me and wanted the best for me, yet I still felt alone. I had dealt with so much on my own that it felt weird to depend on my family. My mother had always been there for us, but it seemed like the older we got, the less she was around. She assumed that she had raised us and that we didn't need her, but that was far from the truth. I needed my mother more than anything and she was never around.

"I feel like I'm drowning and I have a life raft to save me, but I refuse to grab hold of it to save myself."

She leaned back in her seat. "I've been drowning for years. My kids needed me and I chose to stay high over protecting them," she looked away. I could tell speaking about this was causing her to be emotional.

I thought about Chance and how I thought I wasn't hurting him because he wasn't around me all the time. I thought because we lived a few hours away that I wasn't doing harm to him. In reality, I was hurting him more than I knew. He had to live with his mother being 'sick' and not seeing me when he wanted because I was too high to drive, or I couldn't function without getting high before I left. Then, I had Staten who loved everything about me and wanted the best for me. All he wanted was for me to get clean, raise my son and be happy. He wasn't asking for the world, everything he wanted was things to make me and my life better. Instead of appreciating him for all that he was, I fought him and broke up because it was something that I couldn't handle. I couldn't handle looking in his face knowing that I was doing the opposite of what he wanted for me.

I looked ungrateful and selfish when I ended things with Staten and that wasn't the case. The fun and romance of it all had faded. I could see in his face it wasn't the love that kept our relationship going. It was his worry for my sobriety. The dynamic had changed, and I can't blame him for that, it was all me. He went from sexing me in the morning so good that I couldn't walk, to waking up and asking me was I good or if I needed anything. He worried about every and anything that could cause me to relapse. If I complained about the rain, he would give me a look that demanded to know if I was going to get high because I hated the rain. I wanted him to come over to hang with me, not to check my apartment and car for drugs. It went from us falling head over heels for each other to him becoming more like a sober coach. As much as I loved and wanted to be with him, I had to end things between us.

"I don't want to hurt my son. He doesn't deserve that."

"Honey, you've hurt him and I know that. We think we're only hurting ourselves when we're getting high, but we're hurting our children, family and friends. Yes, we're doing the damage to our bodies, but what about the people who have to watch you doing it? My daughters had to sit back and watch every pill I shoved down my throat, even when I wasn't in pain. They had to beg, plead and make bargains for me to get clean. I never listened and each time I chose to put drugs into my body, a small piece of them died."

"How did you do it... I mean, how did you get clean? I tried. It's hard."

"Life is hard. Getting high was the hardest, yet easiest thing I've ever done. Hard because it was all I had known, easy because compared to the life issues I face every day, that was a piece of cake."

"What was the thing that forced you to get clean?"

"Nothing can force you to get clean, babe. You have to want to do it or else it isn't going to work. Being that you have one failed attempt, you know that. I've tried to get clean over a dozen times. I've made promises that I broke and hurt people who I cared for."

"That's what made you get clean?"

"I hurt my babies. I wasn't there to protect them when I should have been. My daughters needed me and I was too worried about getting high."

I leaned back and closed my eyes briefly. Hurting my family was the last thing that I wanted to do. Hurting them was never on the agenda, and I knew I had damage that would always follow soon as they saw my face. I could do good going forward, but all they would remember is me overdosing and almost losing my life. I couldn't blame them because it was my fault for why they would feel that way.

"I hurt a lot of people. It's not that I want to hurt them but getting high is a way to get away from my reality."

"Love, what is so harsh that you need to get so high that you nearly overdosed?"

"Life," I replied. "Does it get easier?"

"Addiction is beautiful to us. We're able to get high to escape our past or reality. However, it's painful to our family. They have to live with the fact that they may receive a phone call that can alter their lives and force them to put us in the ground because of our addiction."

"It's so hard. I try to run from my past and the pain that I still feel to this day."

"Stop using your pain as an excuse and deal with that shit. Don't go to therapy and tell the therapist what she wants to hear. At the end of the day, she still gets paid whether you're honest or not. Go in there and be honest. Work through your shit and heal your relationships. Stop trying to justify your reason for getting high by saying you're in pain. No one ever said it would be easy, so do the work and make it right," she told me.

Everything Evelyn had told me was what I needed to hear.

To see someone who was once where I was brought comfort that I could battle this disease. "Can I ask you a question?"

"Yep."

"What was the main reason that made you want to get clean?"

"Watching another woman raise my baby. Seeing my baby call another woman mommy and having to be alright with that because it was the decision I chose to make. That's what forced me to get and remain clean. As much as I can't get that time back with my baby, I know she's well taken care of and is loved. The plus is being able to raise my grandchildren and rebuild the relationship I ruined with my daughters. Those are things that getting high couldn't give me. In the end, Liberty this is your life and you're going to do what you want. If you're not ready to get clean, the sad reality is that you won't get clean. I pray that almost losing your life is a wake-up call that you need," she told me as she stood up and touched my arm. "If you ever need to talk or anything, you give me a call," she hugged me.

"Thank you, Evelyn. I appreciate you sharing your story with me," I told her. It was true, I meant every word that I had said. Hearing her story had put a lot into perspective for me.

The door opened and Staten walked in with a duffle bag on his shoulder. "Hey Ev," he hugged Evelyn.

"Hey Shaliq... I'm about to head out. Me and your mama was just speaking about you," she smiled up at him.

"What I do now?"

"You need to go visit your mama more, boy. Don't make me go stick Tweeti on you," she teased.

"Man, she always picked on me when we were younger. Don't try and make her do it now," he laughed and hugged her.

"Alright now," she smiled and left out of the room.

The room grew quiet as Staten sat his duffle bag onto the empty hospital chair. My phone buzzed for the first time since I had opened my eyes. I winced as I grabbed my phone and saw Ty's name. I was glad that it was a text message instead of him calling. *How would I explain why my voice sounded like I had swallowed a thousand frogs?*

Haven't heard from you. You good? Been calling and haven't heard anything. His text read.

"How long you've been awake?"

"An hour or so. I was talking to Evelyn."

"Evelyn is good peoples. My mom used to come over to her crib and play cards and shit. My mom stopped because she realized that she was starting to develop a drinking problem by hanging with Ev."

"Good for her."

"Yeah. They reconnected a few years ago and kept in touch."

"She said your mom told her to come speak to me."

"I can see why."

"Yeah, talking to her made everything real for me and put a lot into perspective for me," he sat down and stared at me.

"Waking up in a hospital bed didn't make shit real for you?"

"Here you go," I looked away. He couldn't just have a simple conversation. Staten always had to pick apart my words and second guess them.

"I'm just saying. You could have fucking died and you're telling me that talking to a woman made the shit real for you."

"How do you know I didn't try and kill myself?"

He leaned back in the seat and stroked his beard. "Because I know you. If you wanted to get the job done, you would have."

"Ouch."

"You don't half-ass shit. If you want to get high, you'll get the highest you've ever been," I could hear the sarcasm in his voice, and I didn't like it.

"You don't have to be here. We're not together anymore."

"Liberty, I don't give a damn if we're not together anymore.

Something wrong with you, I'm going to come running because I love you."

"The way you fucked me and left me in that bathroom was the complete opposite of love," I brought up.

After having sex with him, I went home and cried hard. I had never felt so cheap and unloved in my life. Staten had always been the one to show me all the love I needed and at the moment he was so cruel and cold. Hearing him put another woman before me made me want to cry ten times more because I used to be the woman that he would run to.

"You wanted sex and I gave you that. Stop playing the victim like you didn't call for any of this. You wanted us to be over, not the other way around."

"Because you treat me like you're my sober coach. Oh, and because you don't know how to put your baby mama in her place. There's no reason she can do and say whatever she wants, but the moment I choose to say something I'm the fucking problem."

As much as I wanted to blame Staten's sober coach behavior, it was more than that. I didn't want to deal with he and Chanel's weird ass relationship. He acted like she got on his nerves or like he was going to put her in her place, yet he did the exact opposite. He allowed her to be the third part of our relationship. Things happened, which is why I accepted that he had a baby on the way. I could deal with that, but the constant nagging and inserting of Chanel was something that I couldn't deal with, and I shouldn't have to. Each time she got mad about something that had to do with me, she would threaten that Staten couldn't see his daughter when she was born. I didn't want to be the reason he didn't see his daughter or the conflict in their argument so removing myself from our relationship seemed to be the best thing. Of course, looking back it hurt and I hate it had to come to that, but I knew things would change and they would end up being worse.

"If you wanted me to say something to Chanel then you should have said something. Closed mouths don't get fed."

"I shouldn't have to say anything. The disrespect and the barging in on our time was evident. You saw and never said anything. Then, Maliah."

He made a face when I mentioned her name. "What about Maliah?"

"She wants you and you refuse to see that. You kept disregarding my feelings and making me seem like I was crazy."

"No I didn't."

"Okay," I replied.

"You want to point out shit, yet you're the one that was getting high behind my back," he brought up, which I knew he would.

"And I fucked up. All I'm asking is for you to take some responsibility in the shit that you do too."

He sighed.

"You want me to take responsibility but couldn't keep it real with me as to why we broke up. You wanted to hide by needing space instead of being real and at least allowing me the time to fix things," I didn't want to talk anymore. So, I looked out the window and ignored him. "You want shit on your terms and it don't work like that. I fucked you because we're not together and that's what you were begging for. I'm the bad guy though. Not you. I have feelings too and you keep forgetting that because it's all about your fucking feelings," he stood up and pointed at me.

"Well, then stop coming around me."

"Bet. Sayless."

"Less has been said!" I screeched as he closed the door behind me. I was upset because he had come in here and pissed me off in a matter of minutes. How was he pissed because I chose to end things because of his chaotic life? He wanted the option to change things and I wasn't in the mood for that. Staten didn't want to see the shit and I was tired of sticking around praying that he would see it.

FREEDOM HAD CLEANED my entire apartment. It was like I was stepping into a brand-new apartment. My linens, laundry and everything had been washed and put away. My fridge had been cleaned and my living room was switched around. She even changed my balcony carpet and put new furniture out there. She went above and beyond, and I appreciated my twin for it. She could have chosen to be upset and not want to deal with me, yet she came and decided to make life easier for me.

I had been home for a week and I hadn't seen Justice once. Freedom came over every day in the morning to make sure that I was fine. As much as I wished she didn't, I appreciated it because I couldn't take my twin being upset with me. As far as Justice, she hadn't come over, called or sent me a text since I had been home. I was trying not to be in my feelings about it, but I couldn't help it. She had a lot going on with both she and Priest, then she had to be there for Yasmine, so I always managed to talk myself out of sending her a message that I would regret. It was hard trying to get back to regular life and act like nothing happened. I sat the rehab brochures the hospital had gave me with my discharge papers on the coffee table and went to sit on the balcony. I grabbed the carton of cigarettes on the side table before I made my way outside. While I took a long pull of the cigarette, I scrolled my social media to see what I had been missing. It seemed like I hadn't missed much.

When can I see you? A text from Ty popped up on my phone.

I exited out of the third Insta-story I was watching and went to our text message thread. Since he had sent me that text message in the hospital, I hadn't replied to him. *What was I supposed to say? I overdosed and was in the hospital because of it?* That wasn't something I wanted to share with him.

Today. If you're not too busy. I Couldn't lie. I missed seeing his face and I wanted to spend some time with someone that actually didn't know the real me. Me and Staten hadn't spoken since our argument at the hospital. I hoped his new baby with Chanel was keeping him occupied. I understood he cared and that's why a lot of our issues occurred, still, he had to take responsibility for the shit that he did too.

Bet send me your location. I'll come over.

I sent him my address and finished my cigarette. Freedom had an appointment with Samoor, so I knew she wouldn't come over until tomorrow. Since my apartment was cleaned, I didn't need to scramble to toss clothes in the closet to make it seem presentable. Ty had never been to my apartment and I had to admit I was a bit scared. I flicked the rest of the bud off my balcony and dialed Justice's number. It rang for a minute before her sleepy voice came through the line.

"Hello?" she answered.

"Why haven't I seen you?" I knew I should or could have started the conversation better, yet I needed to know.

She sucked her teeth. "I literally just went to sleep. Liberty, I don't have time for this," she complained.

"Answer the question," I was adamant on finding out why I haven't seen my baby sister. When something was wrong Justice was known for keeping her distance. So, I needed to know what her issue with me was.

"Liberty, you have the nerve to call me with this shit!" she raised her voice. "I have a lot going on in my life and the last thing I needed was to find you damn near dead. If you want to shove that shit up your nose, you can do it in the privacy of your own place without me. I refuse to bring my daughter back to that damn place!" she hollered into the phone and ended the call.

I sat looking at my phone. When she spoke, I could hear her voice quivering, which meant I had fucked her up mentally. As much as I was upset about her not coming around me, I had to realize that I put her in a position that she should have never been in. I wiped the tear that fell down my cheek and went to shower and toss some make-up on to look presentable. The dark circles around my eyes weren't cute at all.

Ty arrived nearly an hour later with a bottle of expensive sparkling water, roses and a box of expensive chocolates. I knew they were expensive because I had heard one of the nurses bragging about the chocolate that her husband spent three hundred dollars for. It was stupid when I heard her bragging about it, but right here and now I felt special. He could have just showed up and saw me. Instead, he put time in to making me feel special.

"Let me put these in water," I gently grabbed the flowers from him and went into the kitchen. "You can take a seat on the couch.

"Stop fronting. You know you about to let them die," he joked, which caused me to smile. A smile hadn't come across my face in a few weeks. Well, at least a genuine one hasn't.

"I have a green thumb and I bet next time you see them they'll be alive."

"Oh word? I can come back."

I smirked. "It depends. The night is still early," I grabbed a crystal vase Freedom had gifted me for our birthday a few years ago. It was from Tiffany's and she insisted I be home the day it arrived.

I filled the vase with water, then rummaged through my junk draw for a penny. Tossing the penny into the water, I cut the stems and sat them in the vase. Ty was occupied with his phone while I tended to the flowers. Once I was done, I opened the bottle of water and poured him a glass. He put his phone away when I came into the living room.

"Not thirsty?"

"No." Water was the last thing that I was thinking about. "How have you been? I know busy," I pointed to his phone.

"Me and my cousin are partnering on a hotel and casino in Vegas, so I've been back and forth."

"Vegas, huh? That's a big jump from your hole in the wall in jersey," I smirked.

He turned and faced me, placing the water on the table. "My cousin is big in the real estate development business. Everything he touches turns to gold."

"I can imagine. A business man with some street in him," I watched as he took me in and smiled.

He grabbed my hands and his eyes landed on my hospital band. Out of everything I was checking for, how did I forget that? "What happened?" he demanded to know.

"I fell," I lied.

He looked me in the eyes as if he was searching for the truth. "Tell me the truth. If you want to lie, I can get up and walk out right now. Be honest with me."

Half of me wanted to tell him to leave, then the other part wanted to tell him. I was tired of hiding, lying and not being honest. "I'm an addict."

"I figured from seeing the rehab brochures when I sat down. What's your poison?"

"Coke," I searched his face for a disapproving expression and found none. He continued to stare me in the face. "Look, if you don—"

He pulled his wallet out and took a small gold chip out of it. "I used to be an alcoholic. Got so bad that my family stopped fucking with me. That whole in the wall club you were in, used to be a big thing back in the day. I allowed my drinking to run my business into the ground. I couldn't start my day unless I had three shots of Patron. My cousin stopped fucking with me and all the niggas who I thought were my friends encouraged that shit. One night, I got behind the wheel and drove myself home... I hit a woman and killed her," he revealed. I watched as the pain appeared on his face. You could tell this was a burden that he carried with him. "She was just trying to get home to her six kids. Because I was stupid and drunk, I killed a woman who had kids that need her."

"I never would have guessed that. Did you go to jail?"

"Yeah, I did six months and had to take a bunch of classes. That was six years ago and every month I still send ten thousand a month to her family. It will never be enough to bring their mother back, but it will help."

"That's nice of you. Some people wouldn't have done that."

"Wanna know what fucks me up?"

"What?"

"Her family forgave me. In court at my sentencing, her oldest daughter hugged me and said they forgave me. I sat in that cell that night and cried like a fucking baby."

"Can I hug you?"

"Yeah," I reached my arms around his neck and hugged him so tight. It took a lot to admit all that he had just admitted to me. We hugged for what seemed like hours before we pulled apart. "Whenever I'm having a bad day, or a stressful day, which I have a lot of, the one thing I think of is how good a cold beer or shot of bourbon would taste. Then I look at this coin and think of the family I destroyed because I wanted to drink, and it makes the craving go away. You have to have your *why* when getting clean. It can't be for anyone other than you.

"I overdosed and my baby sister found me on the couch. Getting clean seems so hard when there are so many reasons for me to keep getting high."

"Once you have your *why,* it won't be hard to do anything. Your mental is what's holding you back. When someone wants to do something, they'll do that shit with no questions asked.

Stop holding yourself back. What kind of life has being high given you?"

"A quiet and lonely one," I admitted. My life was quiet and quite lonely for some time. It wasn't until Staten entered that I didn't feel so lonely anymore. With him gone, I was back to being alone all the time.

"Imagine what life would be like if you didn't have to hide who you are. You would be free. It feels nice to get high, but it's a prison. You can't travel because guess what? You can't bring coke with you. Hiding it from your family is a fucking task and it's all you can think about when you're not high."

"That's true," I had to admit.

"I know because that's how that shit used to be with me. When I wasn't drunk, I was thinking about the next time I could get drunk."

It felt freeing to sit and talk to Ty without being judged. He didn't make me feel like I was beneath him. He sympathized with me and made me see things differently.

"Thank you for sharing your story with me."

"Anytime. Now, I want you to tell me something."

"What?"

"Are you planning on going to any of these?"

I shrugged. "I was just looking at them. Oh, and please don't offer to pay for anything," I added.

He chuckled. "I wasn't. If this is what you want, then this is something you need to pay for. If you don't stick it out, then you wasted your own money."

I shoved him. "Whatever," I giggled.

"On the real, do what you feel is right for you. I'm not going to tell you what I think you should do. I want you to do what is best for you. Find your *why* and I promise everything else will fall into place."

"Thanks for this, Ty."

"No problem at all," he looked at his phone. "I gotta

meeting in the city in an hour and a conference call on the way to the meeting. I would stay longer, but I just wanted to see your face while I had some time in-between meetings."

"Busy man. It's fine. I'm going to try and get some sleep anyway."

"Rest up. I'll call you tonight. Maybe I can take you to dinner this week," he stood up and smiled at me.

I wrapped my arms around his neck as he held me tightly. "Maybe," I replied.

"See you soon," he told me and kissed me on the lips. "You got this, ight? God gives his toughest battles to his strongest soldiers."

"I'm starting to believe that."

"Good," he said as his phone started ringing in his hand. "I'll call you," he whispered as he picked up the phone and headed out the door.

I shut the door, grabbed the chocolates and sat on the couch. Whenever I was down, I put my favorite movie on *The Devil Wears Prada* and watched like it was the first time. For the first time, this movie wasn't moving me, and I couldn't focus in on anything. I sighed, turned the TV off and grabbed my phone. I counted to three and dialed a number.

"Renewing Lives Rehabilitation, how may I help you?"

"Hi, my name is Liberty McGurry and I would like to check into your facility."

5

Priest

"Kiki, this is the second time you've been sick this week. Your temperature is fine, and you don't look sick, what's going on?" I asked as she laid under her covers.

This was the second time this week that she complained of being sick. It wasn't like I was missing out on work and money, but I needed to know why she wanted to stay home when she loved school.

"My stomach hurts. I think my period is coming on."

"You're a lie. You had it earlier this month. With what Kiss pulled, I'm on top of your periods," I revealed.

"Ro, that's creepy."

"I'll be the creepy uncle then. I don't need no more babies being brought up in here. Go and get dressed so I can take you to school," I tapped her leg and left the room.

Doing all of this without Justice was like back to normal. Except, I had a crazy little great-nephew crawling and trying to walk. Kiss helped when she wanted and that wasn't often. When Justice was here, things ran smoother. Even if we had a bad day, I was happy to climb in bed with her at the end of the day. Laying in my empty bed at night felt like torture. Especially since I could smell her on the pillows and sheets. We ate out all the time and missed Justice singing off key as she worked around the kitchen. It seemed like all I missed was what she did around the house and that was the furthest from the truth. I missed having someone to vent to , lay with and laugh with too.

She hated me. I could tell whenever she looked at me. When I came up to see our daughter, she barely uttered three words to me. Everything about our encounters were so cold. A woman who had a smile that could melt a snowman, now became as cold as ice. It was me who made her that way. My selfish decision making was what landed us in this situation from jump. I wish I could have blamed someone. Instead, I had to take that L and try to fix the heart I had shattered. There was nothing I could do that would make up for missing our daughter's birth, however I could try and be there for them every step of the way.

"Boy, stop messing with that trash," Kiss yawned as she made her some coffee. Zamari crawled behind his mother in hopes of her picking him up off the floor.

"Where did you go last night?"

"Reese gave me some money for diapers, and we were sitting outside talking."

"He knows Zamari not his, right?"

She rolled her eyes. "You had a problem when I was in your pockets, and now I'm in Reese's pockets you just have to ask questions."

"My point was to be in your own pockets, not a nigga's pocket. Go back to school or something, Kiss." This seemed to be an ongoing argument every morning between us.

"Here we go again with this," Love sighed as she entered the kitchen. She grabbed the bagels I grabbed down the street and took a bite out of it.

"You did something new with your hair?"

"Yeah. I dyed it brown three weeks ago. Thanks for noticing, Ro," she cut her eyes at me. She and Kiss made some weird eye contact before Love headed to the door.

"Go wait in the car, Kiki is getting ready."

"I'm going to school with my friends. They're picking me up this morning. Oh, and I'm going to the library afterschool."

"Alone?" Kiss asked.

"Why is it your business? You should be taking care of your child," she snapped and headed out the door.

"You better get your niece. She got one more time to mention my son and I'm gonna beat her ass," Kiss waved the spoon in the air. "She think she too good because she don't have a baby or something?"

"Why couldn't your mother have three boys? She just had to have three girls nearly back to back," I sighed. "Kiki!"

"I threw up!" she yelled back.

"Kiki, you're going to school tomorrow and I don't care if you're bleeding out of your eyeballs!" I yelled back.

"Heard you!" she replied and slammed her door behind her.

I leaned back in the chair and sent Justice a quick text message. *What time you going to see Yasmine?*

Usual time.

Can we talk after?

For?

Come on, Jus.

She never replied back. That was the norm when it came to our text messages. I would initiate the text and she would only entertain the message for so long before she never replied back.

"How's Yaya doing?"

"You insist on calling her that, huh?"

"Yep." Kiss handed Zamari a piece of the bagel and he finally sat still and tried to figure out how he was going to demolish the piece with only three teeth. "I like how it sounds."

"She's doing good. Eating more ounces but haven't been able to keep her temperature outside of the incubator. I hate seeing her like that."

"Me too. It will get better and she'll be home before you know it."

"Yeah, it's which home that worries me."

"Well, you know it won't be this one. Justice is done with you and for good reason too," she took a sip of her coffee.

"You my niece, right?"

"Uh huh. I'm also a woman and what you did was wrong. If it was me, I would have shot you, but Justice is taking the nice approach to this."

I shook my head. "How do I fix this?"

"I don't know. Maybe it's not fixable. You hurt her when she told you that she didn't want to be hurt anymore. Lavern was nice when we were younger, but she' not the same person she was years ago and you're not either. Why throw away all of this for something old?"

"Cause I'm a fool," I admitted.

"Clearly. It's going to be hard to try and repair what you broke. She already had a broken heart and trusted you. That wall is going to be ten times harder to break down, if you can even break it down."

Kiss usually spoke about bullshit, so I tuned her out. This morning she made a point and was right with everything she had said. Justice let me in while getting her heart broke by her ex. She told me her fears and why she was hesitant about letting me in. Despite her fears, she let her guard all the way down and allowed me in. What did I do? I fucked that up and ruined what we had.

"I just want to make the shit right with her. I fucking miss the shit out of her."

"Bet you do. What about Lavern? I'm sure she's missing you too."

"It's nothing with me and Lavern. We fucked and that was it."

"She knows that?"

"Kiss don't you have a baby to take care of?"

"Y'all keep bringing my son up and I'm gonna fight you all in here," she rolled her eyes and grabbed Zamari up.

"Yeah, go and raise that baby," I continued to tease her.

"Go to hell, Ro!" she hollered as she walked up the stairs.

I laughed and cleaned the kitchen so I could head to the hospital. As much as Justice didn't want to talk, we had to talk about our future with Yasmine. Despite what we were going through, we needed to have a plan for when Yasmine came home from the hospital. After checking in on Kiki, who was asleep, I showered and got dressed before I headed out.

It didn't take me long to make it to the hospital. I pulled into the maternity assigned parking spots and sat in the car for a minute. It was like no one wanted me to have a minute to myself because as soon as I leaned my head back on the chair, my phone started to ring. Lavern's name flashed across my car's screen and I sighed. It wasn't that I was pissed with Lavern, it was that I needed to focus on rebuilding my relationship and family, and I couldn't have them both.

"What's good, Lavern?" I answered the phone.

"Hi, haven't heard from you in a little while... are we good?" she asked.

I had been distant when it came to me and Lavern. With Yasmine being born early, me hurting Justice and trying to keep the girls together, I didn't have time to lay up and chill. Shit, I didn't even want to lay up with her anymore. Seeing that look on Justice's face made me want to stop the bullshit and get my shit together. The pain etched on her face made me hurt ten times more. What hurt the most was that whenever she thought of our daughter's birth, she would think of our relationship going to shit. Yasmine's birth was supposed to be a special day for the both of us and all she'll remember is that I missed it and she had to have Ghost step in for me.

"We're good. I just been handling a lot so I haven't had a minute to check in with you," I replied as I killed my engine and stepped outside the car.

"I understand. How's your daughter doing?"

"She's good."

"Ro, why are you being so short with me? Are we really alright?" she asked for the second time. I knew she could tell from my tone that I didn't want to be on the phone. And, it wasn't anything against her personally. My mind had been all over, and I didn't have the time to sit and explain everything to her.

"We're good, Lavern," I spotted Justice getting off the bus from across the street. "I gotta go. I'm visiting my daughter. I'll hit you up later," I promised, knowing that I would probably forget.

"Can we meet up for lunch this week to talk? I just really miss you and want to see you. I can book our suite at the hotel."

"Yeah," I replied. "Talk to you soon," I ended the call and sprinted across the hospital's campus until I reached Justice.

She had headphones on and when she saw me, she offered me a weak smile. I was surprised she took one headphone out and stepped to the side so the nurses starting their shift could enter the hospital.

"Good morning," I felt like a shy little boy trying to talk to Justice. All the nights that I was up inside her guts flashed through my mind. I would give anything to make love and show her how much I loved her and fucked up.

"Morning. What did you want to talk about?"

"Let me take you to breakfast. The nurses are making their rounds, so you know we'll have to wait in the waiting room while they do their rounds with every baby in there," she knew what I was saying was true.

"I guess."

I showed her back to my car and held the door open. It felt like I was in high school and had got my dream girl to go to prom with me. "I thought you were holding onto Staten's whip."

"I gave it back to him. Getting around on the bus is fine."

"Nah, use one of my cars. You're gonna need it."

"I'm fine, Priest."

I decided not to push because I knew my ass was on thin ice with her ass. I was lucky she agreed to even come to breakfast with me. There was a small diner near the hospital, so I ended up going there. We both had come here to grab food whenever we were staying with Yasmine overnight since it was opened 24/7. Soon as we walked in, we were seated in a booth near the bar. Justice pulled her phone out and sent a few text messages while I took in her beauty.

"You can stop staring at me," she said, not bothering to look up from the phone. "What did you want to talk about?"

The waitress came and took our orders before she left to go put them in. "What's going to happen when Yasmine gets released out of the hospital? I don't want you sleeping on every-body's couch with my daughter."

She chuckled. "Why are you so worried?"

"Yasmine is my daughter too, Justice. What's going on between us doesn't have anything to do with her... feel me?"

She nodded her head. "You're right. I have an apartment that I'm moving into the end of the month. We'll be fine."

"Come back home, Jus," I slipped and pleaded. I wanted her to come back more than anything in the world. The house didn't feel the same and knowing that Yasmine wouldn't come home with me made me feel like shit.

"That's not my home. Let's be honest, that was you and the girls' home, and I just moved in. Priest, I don't ever want to come back to that house again. Before you did what you did, living with you was hell. You ignored me and refused to speak to me because I had said something you didn't like."

"Ma, I love you and want to fix what I did to you and Yasmine. All I want is my family back and under one roof. If I need to buy another house, I'll do that shit."

"Shouldn't you be catching up for lost time with Lavern? Isn't that what you wanted all along?"

I lowered my head and then looked into her eyes. "I'm not making an excuse for what I did, bu—"

"The moment you add a but, you're about to make an excuse for what you did. I'm not asking for an explanation as to why you cheated on me while I was pregnant, all I'm saying is stand behind that shit. You did what you wanted and didn't give a damn about my feelings, so don't try and act like you care now," she accepted the coffee from the waitress and poured some sugar into the cup.

"I fucked up; I know that. If I could reverse the hands on the clock and change what I did, I would. I want to make things right because I want to be with you, Justice. I let an old relationship throw me off track and I apologize for that shit. Hurting you was never the goal and I hate that I did that shit to you. You came into my life and made me feel what it felt like to live again. The way you love me and also accepted my nieces made me feel like I hit the jackpot of women. You not only love hard, but you go to bat for the people that you love and care for. I just want to make it right between us," I touched her hands and she removed them from my grasp.

"You decided that bitch and her history with you was more important than our life that we were building together. I told you to talk to her and square things away, I even asked if she was an issue and you lied and told me that she wasn't. If that wasn't enough, you tried to use our issues we were going through to run to her and do what you did. So, no I don't accept your apology because it's full of shit," she pointed her finger at me. "And can you please put that in a to-go box?" she told the waitress and went to stand by the bar.

"Justic—"

"There's nothing left for us to speak about."

"What about Yasmine?" I held onto her arm because I didn't want her to go.

She sucked her teeth. "Yasmine is your daughter and I will never keep her from you. She'll be able to come spend nights with you and stuff like that. But who are you kidding? This meeting wasn't about Yasmine because you know I would never keep her away from you. You wanted to plead your case in hopes that I would be a fool and take you back."

"Ma, you know I love you and want this more than anything."

"You didn't want this when you were sticking the dick that was meant for me inside a ghost from your past. Priest, stop wasting my damn time and leave me the hell alone," she snatched her hand away, grabbed the bag the waitress was handing her and headed out the door. I leaned my head back on the chair and prayed that I could fix the coldness I had put in her heart.

WITH ALL I had going on, it had been a week since I had been able to get up with Lavern. She was pissed because she had booked a suite and I hadn't been able to show up. My mind wasn't in the right space to sit there and act like I wanted to fuck her, because I didn't. My mind was always on Justice and how I could fix everything I had done to destroy what we had. She didn't deserve what I had done to her and I wanted to fix it more than anything. Lavern had asked me to meet her at some café a few blocks down from her house. I wasn't in the mood to talk about shit, or for her to feel like I'm ignoring her. We never established that we were together or going to be together. We both knew I was involved with someone and that what we were doing was sex; nothing more. The fact that she was pissed, blowing my phone up and shit because I had been busy made me not want to even come to this café. However, since I had been ignoring her, I owed it to her to let her know that I couldn't continue what I had started with her.

Come to my apartment. I'm not ready yet. Lavern sent me a text just as I was pulling up to the café.

I pulled out the spot and headed up the block to her apartment. When I jumped out, a few little niggas nodded as I walked into the building. When I got to her floor, I tapped and stepped back. Lavern opened the door with a silk robe tied around her waist. A part of me felt like she was going to try and pull some shit like this, which is why I was good with meeting at the café.

"This morning has been a shit show. My boss called me in to work this morning, and then my daughter's father was late picking her up. I'm just so tired from all of this," she walked down the hall to her bedroom.

"Yeah, my morning has been a little crazy too," I lied. For the first time, everything ran smoothly between me and the girls. Kiki even got up and went to school without any issues.

"Come back here," she called from her bedroom and I was hesitant. Sex wasn't on my mind and I didn't want to hear her complain when I turned her down.

I walked to the back and found her curling her hair in the mirror. She pointed to the bed, and I sat down and continued to watch her. "What time you gotta be to work?"

"In two hours. He says somebody called out and I could use the hours, so I'm gonna go, even though I don't want to."

"Make that money."

She stopped curling her hair, and then looked at me. "I know I keep asking this, but are we okay? I feel like the vibe is off."

"Justice found out about us."

She looked up at the ceiling. "I know something had to be going on. How did she take it?"

I looked at Lavern like she had lost her mind. "How do you think she took it? I cheated on her while being pregnant."

"She wasn't making you happy anymore. I could tell from the way you would toss your clothes on the floor and climb into bed with me."

I had never told Lavern that Justice wasn't making me happy because that wasn't the truth. Me and Justice happened to be in a weird place when me and Lavern started to fuck around. Never once did I tell her that I wasn't happy.

"I never said I wasn't happy."

She walked over to me and wrapped her arms around me. "I could tell. This wasn't what any of us planned, but we have so much history together."

I removed her hand from me and stood up. "Lavern, we can't continue this. Seeing how much I hurt Justice got me fucked up. It made me realize that I want to be with her and fix what I did."

She took a step back and stared at me for a moment before she opened her mouth to speak. "You get my feelings involved just to tell me that you want to fix it and be with her? Where is that fair to me?"

"Vern, I always wanted to be with Justice. I let what we used to have fuck with my future with Justice and I regret that. We're both not the same people anymore and I was trying to keep something that had felt familiar to me. The truth of the matter is that we're not the same anymore. What we had was when we were younger. I have responsibilities and you do too. Being together or trying to make something happen between the both of us is like trying to start something new, which isn't what I want to do. Justice has my heart."

She folded her arms as tears fell down her cheeks. "We laugh so much, have a good time and have amazing sex. You're acting like all of this was forced onto you or some shit."

I sighed because she wasn't getting what I was saying. "I'm telling you I can't do this anymore. I'm chasing feelings I had in college when I have real shit and a real woman that loves me. I hurt her and all she has ever done was love the shit out of me. I'm man enough to admit I was wrong for what I did to Justice and all I want to do is work hard on fixing that shit between us."

"You're man enough to work on admitting what you did to her, but what about me? What about us? You come into my life, lift my spirits and then leave when shit gets complicated."

"It was fucked up for me to go and get your feelings involved knowing I wanted to be with Justice. Let's not act like we weren't two adults who knew what we were getting ourselves into."

"I know exactly what I was getting myself into. Another man who got pussy and wants to call it quits. Ro, you can just let yourself out. I wish you and your girlfriend the best, considering you have a sick child together, but just stay away from me."

"Sick child? My daughter isn't fucking sick," I got pissed with her saying that shit to me. Yasmine wasn't fucking sick and for her to put that shit out there like it was true pissed me off.

"Whatever. Just get the fuck out of my house."

"You definitely changed. The old Lavern was on my dick because I broke up with her."

"That Lavern died the minute you told me you had another

bitch in your apartment while you kept me in the hallway. A lot has changed for me, some for the good and some for the bad, but one thing I refuse is to let a nigga do me anyway that he wants to, no matter how much I love him," she reached up and mushed me in the head. "Get out of my apartment and don't come back!" she yelled.

"Say no more," I replied. She didn't have to say that shit more than once for me to dip out of her crib.

Lavern had the game fucked up if she thought I was going to call it quits with Justice to be with her. She had some weird ass issues with her future ex-husband, and I didn't need that static. She definitely changed and life had put her through some things. I think it was the thought of having someone who was just as close to Sandy as I was around that caused me to fuck up. I walked around like everything was good, but it was moments like this that I missed the shit out of my big sister. I needed her here with me to help guide me through so much shit that was going on in my life. She was missing out on being a grandmother, being there for both Love and Kiki. Shit, she was missing out on being an auntie and witnessing me being a father to my daughter. I wished like hell I could have introduced Justice to her because she would have fallen in love with her.

I'm sorry. Can we talk again? Lavern text me soon as I entered the car.

Nah, we're good. Be well, Vern. I replied back. This back and forth shit she thought she was gonna do, wasn't going to work. I didn't have time to say sorry, get mad and make up again. When she mentioned my child and called her sick, she fucked up royally with me. I wished like hell I didn't fuck up what I had with Justice for her. Kiss's name popped on the screen, so I hit the green talk icon and pulled out of the parking spot.

"Ro, you need to get to the hospital. Kiki was just rushed there for trying to kill herself!" Kiss was hysterical.

My heart was pumping out of my chest and it felt like I couldn't breathe. My hands were clammy and I felt like my breathing became shallowed. "Kill... herself?" I stammered.

"She was found inside the girl's bathroom at school hanging, Ro. I'm on my way there with Zamari!" she continued to scream.

"Whi...which hospital?" I hollered.

"Staten Island Hospital!" she yelled and the line went dead.

6

Ghost

"You're reacting well to the treatments. We're hopeful that you'll be in remission soon," my doctor informed me.

On a day like today when I felt like I didn't have the energy to even breathe, hearing those words meant everything to me. Instead of trying to be the tough guy, I did everything my doctor told me to do. My mother even had me on a plant-based diet and all these vitamins she had been researching. The only downside of everything was the side effects of chemo. My fucking hair was coming out in clumps and I was so weak I couldn't do anything for days. Shit, I couldn't even fuck the shit out of Free if I wanted to. My dick didn't seem to fucking work and I was getting tired of her rubbing her ass on me before we went to bed and not being able to do anything. I wanted to blow her back out like no other and because I couldn't that shit had me frustrated every night.

The one good thing that happened was Samoor. His heart

condition hadn't worsened, and everything seemed to be going good with him. Free went back to work and was doing a couple hours every day just to get out the house. Ms. Winnie continued to help with the kids. She had been a god send when it came to helping around the house and with the kids. I was happy that Free decided to go back to work. She had expressed that she didn't want to put her career on the back burner because of my life, like she had done in the past. With everything going on, she couldn't help but to put it on the back burner, so when she decided to tell me about going back to work, I was excited for her. I wanted her to get back to some sense of normalcy. Life had been pulling us in all different directions. God was definitely testing us, and I knew it. Being that we were able to try and see the sunlight at the end of the tunnel, made everything worth it.

"I just want to get this shit out of me," I admitted. "My body doesn't feel the same and I'm tired of being tired all the time."

"I can understand that. This treatment approach that we have been taking is working and we'll continue with it for the next few months. I see the end coming and I want to continue on this path, so you can ring that bell out in the hall," she touched my shoulder. "Any more questions?"

"No, I'm good."

"Okay, well keep up with the medications at home and try and get some rest. You look like you're about to fall asleep or something," she giggled.

"Will do. I'm having lunch with Freedom, so I'll nap whenever I get home," I promised and headed out of the office.

I decided I was going to pop up at Free's office and bring some lunch. With everything we had been going through, it felt nice to have a moment where we could connect without the kids. I grabbed some food from our favorite Chinese place and headed to her office. Free's team greeted me when I walked through the door. I knew she was in her office because that's where she spent all her time. Her assistant smiled at me as I kept heading to the back. Free was bent over her design table going over a concept for a room in one of her client's house. I came up behind her and stole a kiss on her neck.

"Hey baby, what are you doing here?" she turned and wrapped her arms around my neck. Free snuck a few more kisses on my lip. "Ugh, you so damn fine," she complimented.

"Nah, you fine. What you working on?"

"Just some music room for my client. Her son plays the piano and she wants a room for him to be able to take lessons and stuff," she explained. "Honestly... she's driving me nuts."

"So, you need a break?" I smirked.

"A much needed one," she smiled and walked over to the seating area in her office. "I see food from my favorite place," she opened the bags and placed it on the table.

"It's good that you're back to work. You need someone else to get on your nerves other than being home stressing."

"I like being home because I can be there for both you and Samoor."

"We pay Ms. Winnie a lot of money to make sure the kids are good. Hell, she even makes sure that I'm good."

"She's great, isn't she?"

"Yeah, I love how she is with the kids."

She handed me my carton of broccoli and garlic sauce, and then sat down across from me. "It makes things easier. How are you feeling? How was your appointment?"

"She said she can see me going into remission in the next few months. So, she doesn't want to switch anything that we're doing right now."

"Oh my God. I'm so excited, so does she know when exactly or..." Freedom got excited and I knew I should have waited to share this news with her. She would be obsessed with knowing when it would happen, and it wasn't something that was definite right now.

"Babe, we don't know all that right now. All she said was that everything is looking good, I don't want you to be so stressed and worried about when it might happen, because it might not happen. Shit can always change."

"I understand, but I don't want to speak anything negative about it not being able to work. God is going to give us a second chance," she took a spoonful of shrimp fried rice into her mouth.

"I hear what you're saying, but don't get your hopes up and start worrying... ight?"

"Yeah, yeah, yeah. Besides that, what else is going on with you? We haven't got a chance to just talk like this in a long time."

"I know. I'm good. Staten is handling everything, and I'm not worried about nothing except beating this cancer, loving you and our kids."

"And being a snooty vegan," she giggled.

"You can be one too."

"Nope. I like meat and all kinds of other stuff that isn't vegan, but I support you and will try to cook more vegan meals."

"Uh huh," I laughed because she was full of crap. Freedom would sit at the table and eat a damn burger before she would eat a vegan meal. I didn't mind either, this was my lifestyle, not theirs. I couldn't front like I didn't want a damn steak or something. My moms did her research, so I trusted her with this whole plant-based lifestyle.

"Anyway, we need to get away for a few days... just me and you," she suggested.

"I'm down. Where you wanna go?"

"I don't care. I feel like we need a getaway to reconnect. And, I've been doing research on something to help with down there," her eyes narrowed in to my crotch area of my pants.

"The fuck you mean you been doing research?"

"Babe, there is some pill that can help with it."

"Viagra, Free?" I put my food down because she had me fucked up if she thought I was about to take that shit.

"No, it's natural. I actually had it sent to the office," she got up and went behind her desk and pulled out a box. "There's a natural website that sells all kinds of natural things. I miss getting dick and I know you miss hitting this," she patted the front of her jeans.

I laughed because she was right. Being able to break her back and make her scream my name sent shutters through my soul. It also frustrated me because I knew the damage I could do when my shit was working.

"I'm not trying that shit."

"Fine," she plopped back down on the couch and picked her food back up. "I want you to know that I'm tired of using my vibrator in the bathroom when you're sleep. I'm not complaining because I know all that you're going through. But, I also know that you could use some relief too."

"Yeah, you right about that," I agreed because I had been backed up, but couldn't do shit about it. My dick wouldn't work and my doctor told me she couldn't tell me exactly when it would start working, so I was screwed.

"Anyway, I'm thinking we should go to Jamaica for a little vacation. We both can use it and the kids can stay with Ms. Winnie."

"Ain't your mom still in Jamaica?"

"No, she's somewhere else. I couldn't hear when she called last week," she rolled her eyes. "Why are you looking at me like that?"

"When is your mom coming back to the states? Does she know about Liberty?"

"Yeah, and she says that she's grown and needs to get her life in order. My mom is enjoying her life and doesn't care what is going on with us."

"That's fucked up. She got grandkids that she doesn't see, and a grandkid she hasn't even met yet. You not going to talk to her about it?"

"I have and she tells me the same thing over and over again."

"And that is?"

"That after our father was killed, she spent so much time putting everything into us that she didn't have anything for herself, so she's here for us when we need her, but she's going to continue her traveling like she promised to herself."

Free's mom went from being involved to just packing a bag and flying from country to country. As much as Free acted like it didn't bother her, it did and I could tell. It wasn't like she could just get on the phone and call her mom because it all depended on the country and if her phone had service. I thanked God for my mother because it didn't matter how much shit we put her through, she was there when it mattered the most. She made sure to spend as much time with the kids. She was in her feelings when we hired Ms. Winnie to care for the kids and the house. As much as she did for us, I couldn't have her doing everything for the house and the kids.

"You need to sit down and have a conversation with her soon. You and your sisters need her, and she's busy living her best life."

"I managed without her in Atlanta, I can do the same here. Liberty is going to be fine and I'm going to make sure of it."

"What's going on with her?"

A big smile came across her face. "She checked herself into rehab. It's a two-month program where she lives in home, and then she'll be released after two months to continue out-patient treatment."

With my eyebrows raised, I looked at her. "Did she check herself in, or did you?"

"She called me from the place earlier this week and told

me. I went by her place and she packed clothes and all her things. I think this was a wake-up call for her to get her shit together."

"What about her and Staten?"

"I don't think they're speaking. Something happened at the hospital and she won't speak about it. Staten has his own life he needs to focus on, and so does Liberty. What is meant to be will be."

"I agree."

"Plus, he needs to be focused on his baby girl and trying to keep his baby mama in check." Free rolled her eyes. "Why did he have to have a baby with her?"

"Same question I ask myself. I don't have to like his baby mama to build a relationship with my niece."

"Chanel will make it nearly impossible for us to see the baby."

"Staten needs to stop being a pussy and let her know what it is. He acts like he's scared of her or some shit," I vented.

Chanel did whatever the fuck she wanted because Staten allowed that shit. Not once did he sit her ass down and tell her how it was going to be. She didn't have no damn money and everything she spent was from his pockets. Chanel had a good job, but she couldn't afford the shit she bought for their daughter. Then, I heard she was shopping for a new condo because she didn't want to move back into her other one. Last time Staten tried to get her to move, she fought him on it. Now, she had some change of heart and was looking at million-dollar properties. We had money, yet at the rate this bitch was trying to spend it, he wouldn't have none left to actually raise his daughter with.

"I agree. She'll keep that baby away and use it as a pawn so Staten can do what she wants. The fact that your mother has been asking to see the baby, and she has blown her off-"

"Wait, what?"

"Yeah, your mother has been wanting to see Satin, and Chanel has basically without saying anything, told her no. Each time your mother reaches out there is some excuse as to why she can't come over or bring the baby over."

"I don't even know why you told me that. Shit like that pisses me the fuck off," I put my food onto the table. I had lost my appetite and didn't feel like talking about this shit.

"Don't go and get involved in your brother's business. As much as we hate how he's handling things, it's not our business," she warned me.

If I was handling shit, my hand would have been wrapped around Chanel's throat as I told her how shit would be. But, because Staten was a grown man, I was going to allow him to do shit his way. In the end, I prayed that he got this shit in check before I had to say something to ol' girl.

MY BROTHERS MEANT a lot to me, so I knew that I needed to get up and see what was good with them. Today was a good day, so I wanted to be around them while I was feeling up to it. Staten told me he was home, so I called Priest and told him to meet me over here. I pulled into the driveway and entered the house. Staten was in the kitchen making a bowl of cereal when I arrived. He nodded at me and then came over and hugged me quickly. I could tell he was tired and had a lot going on.

"You looking good," he complimented. "How you feeling?" he followed up.

"I have my good and bad days."

"What type of day is today?" Priest asked walking through the door. I could tell something was wrong because he didn't look like himself.

"Don't worry about me, what's good with you?" I asked, as I hugged him.

He sighed and took a seat in the living room. "Kiki tried to kill herself in school," he revealed. Staten dropped the spoon he held in his hand.

"Why the fuck didn't you tell us? How and when this shit happen?" I asked, worried about Kiki.

"Ghost, we all got a lot of shit going on and I didn't need to add that onto anyone's plate. It happened last week," he revealed.

"And you didn't think to tell any of us?" Staten left his table on the counter and came and sat beside me.

"Man, a lot been happening and I was trying to keep every-thing under control. That shit scared the fuck out of me, so I'm sorry if I didn't think to call y'all," he stood up and started pacing the floor.

"Nah, we're family and wanted to be there for you both," I told him. "How is she doing?" I had been around Kiki since she was damn near a baby. To hear that she tried to kill herself killed a piece of me because I looked at the girls like my little sisters.

"She's home and resting. I pulled her out of school for the rest of the year. I'm gonna find a tutor who can come to the house and make sure she is up to speed on work."

"Did she tell you why?"

"Fucking bullying, man. Them pale ass fucking crackers at her school pick on her about everything. The boys even do shit to her and she couldn't take it."

"I hate when they say that words don't hurt because that shit do. Some of the most hurtful shit to happen to me was with words," Staten said.

"Word," I agreed.

"Justice knows?"

"Nah."

"Don't you think she should know?"

"Nah," he replied being short. I could tell he was shutting down and didn't want to talk about this anymore.

"You know just because she's upset doesn't mean that she stopped caring. Those girls mean just as much to her too."

"I don't want to talk about this anymore."

"How's Yasmine?" Staten switched the subject.

"Last I spoke to the doctor; she was doing good. They want to perform some more test on her, since she was born early to make sure everything is still good."

"That's good. And Lavern?"

"I ended shit with her. If me and Justice gonna have a chance, I knew I couldn't do it with her around."

"And she took that fine?"

"Nah, she got Justice's number and been calling and texting her. When she told me, I couldn't even focus because my mind was on Kiki."

"Damn...," I whistled. Priest didn't mean any harm when he started fucking around with Lavern. I knew he was chasing a memory and thought it would be the same. While acting in his own selfishness, he didn't see the harm and pain he was bringing to Justice until it was too late. It only took one mistake, and he learned that his one mistake cost him the love of his life. I prayed that the both of them could come back together and make their relationship work. Not even for the sake of Yasmine, but for the both of them. Justice loves Priest, and he loves her too.

"Enough about me? How's everything?" he looked at me.

"I'm good. Today."

"That's what counts, right?"

I smiled. "Yep."

"And you?" he looked at Staten.

"Maliah's pregnant."

"The fuck you mean Maliah's pregnant?" Priest asked.

He leaned back on the couch and sighed. "Me and Maliah has been fucking around, and Messiah knows," he decided to lay everything out onto the table.

"How are you even here to tell us this shit? If Messiah knew, she would have tried to kill you."

He did a nervous chuckle. "She kind of did."

"How did you end up fucking with Maliah? I can't believe this shit, and then you got her pregnant?" I looked at my younger, dumb brother. *How did he always end up in these situations?*

"Me and her had a vibe and started fucking around in Belize. Getting pregnant wasn't the plan, but she got pregnant and wants to keep it."

"Let me guess.... You don't want the baby, right?" Priest guessed.

"Nah, I'm excited for the baby. Maliah isn't no silly hoe who I wouldn't want to have my baby. She got her head on screw straight, so I know she will be a good mother."

"Nigga, her own mother wasn't even a good mother. She had those girls committing murder before they were old enough to drive. How you think the maternal side gonna kick in for her?" Priest plopped down on the couch just as confused as I was.

"It's done and there is no going back. Messiah isn't happy about the shit, but Maliah is pushing back, so her mother has no choice but to accept shit."

"No choice and Messiah in the same sentence?" I asked. Messiah had plenty of choices and all of them included Staten's ass being shot in the street. She was allowing Maliah and Staten to do their thing because of the love she had for her daughter.

"Yeah, I'm not even stressing that right now. Chanel mad because I won't give her the bread for this condo by the beach. It's five minutes from mommy, but I'm not buying that shit."

All I could do was shake my head because Chanel had some nerve to be pissed. He could buy her a damn box and she should be appreciative. "And what you told her?"

"I told her that I wasn't buying that condo. If she wants to move, fine, but it's not going to be in no damn multi-million-dollar condo."

"So, because of that you're not allowed to see Satin?"

"Nope. It's sad that I don't even have a bond with my own daughter. Any little thing and Chanel withholds her from me," he admitted.

"You still let her do what she wants, so none of that matters," I added.

"What you want me to do? Knock down her parent's door and take my daughter?"

"Yeah, if that would help. We saw that baby once she was born and haven't seen her since. Mommy been wanting to see her and reaching out, but Chanel keeps playing."

"Shit, I can't even see my own seed, so I damn sure can't help none of y'all," he shook his head and put his hand over his face. "I'm trying to do my best and it still don't seem like it's enough. Then, she keep bringing up us having another baby."

"Nigga, if you get her pregnant again, you stupid," Priest raised his voice and pointed at Staten.

"I'm not doing that shit. Chanel ass drove me crazy enough with one pregnancy, you think I'll do that shit again? Hell nah."

"Lie to her," I blurted.

"Huh?" both he and Priest said.

"She wants something, right? Lie and tell her that you're down for baby number two. You'll get to see the baby, and she thinks you're down to make baby number two."

"Smart," he replied.

"And what is going on with you and Maliah? You gonna get into a relationship with her?" I wondered out loud.

"We're taking it slow."

"Liberty know?" Priest questioned.

"Nah. She got her own issues and don't need to be worried about mine right now."

I sighed because my brother always managed to get his ass into some sort of trouble. This time, I couldn't help him out. We sat and chilled for a bit before I headed home to take a nap. It seemed like all my ass did was sleep, but it was well needed. I wanted to be awake with the kids got home so we could watch a movie together or something before Freedom got off from work.

7

Maliah

"I'm tired all the damn time. I be in the trap house knocked the hell out," I laughed as I laid across my sister's couch.

"Pregnancy will do that to you. How has Staten been handling it?"

I shrugged my shoulders. "I wouldn't know. We haven't seen much of each other lately. In passing, he makes sure I'm good, but he hasn't come over to my house and I haven't been over to his," I admitted.

A month had passed and I was now officially twelve weeks pregnant. I was excited because I never thought I wanted to be a mother. The small changes to my body excited me. Being tired, hungry and cranky all the time wasn't something I enjoyed, still I couldn't complain. Staten came to my appointments when he wasn't busy and I didn't mind that he missed some. We didn't need to go to every single one together. Besides eating and sleeping, I held up my end of the deal with my mother. Work was still getting done and I hadn't been slacking on anything. My mother wasn't happy about the pregnancy and made sure to let me know each time she saw me. My father on the other hand was excited to become a grandfather. He told me it would take my mother some time to wrap her head around it, but once she did, she would love my baby too. While he saw the positive, I knew my mother and knew if shit didn't go her way, she would never come around to anything.

Staten had been busy and I knew Chanel had been giving him hell. I tried to be the baby mother that didn't get on his nerves and did her own thing. It wasn't like I needed him for everything. The only thing I missed was feeling him, sliding up inside of me at night, or wrapping his arms around me. Still, I wasn't going to nag and beg him to spend time with me. Whenever he had time in his schedule, I prayed he would fit me in. In the meantime, I was excited to be having a baby and getting prepared for all of the things that a baby would need. I wished I had my mother to talk to about it. She refused to even acknowledge that I was pregnant. If I didn't have my father or twin, I probably would have felt alone and would have become clingy to Staten. Since I had them, I didn't feel the need to always be around him.

"What are the both of you going to do as far as relationship?" Mariah looked at me as she polished her toes.

"We're not thinking about that. Our main focus is this baby. A relationship may come, or it may not."

"And what about Liberty?"

"What about her?" I hated that Mariah always felt the need to bring her up. It didn't matter what we were talking about it when came to Staten, she always found a way to slip Liberty's name in there. I didn't see the reason to always mention someone he was no longer with anymore.

"You really think he's just going to give up being with her for you?"

"I'm not asking him to give up anyone for me. They broke up before me and him even got together."

"You don't think he'll get back with her?"

"Time will only tell if he would. Being that she decided to start using again, I highly doubt that he will."

"Love is love," Mariah added. "It doesn't matter if she sniffed the whole baby powder section in Target. If he loves her, he'll make exceptions and be with her."

"Why do you insist on telling me this?"

"Because the last thing I want is for you to get hurt. I can see you're all wrapped into him, but is he feeling the same way?"

Mariah pissed me off when she did this. It was like she wanted me to be angry with Staten because we hadn't spent time together. How could I be mad at him? I lived the same life and time wasn't always on our side when it came to spending time with the people that mattered the most. Mariah didn't understand because she shopped and waited hand and foot on her boyfriend. She accepted any small window of time he gave her and was fine with that. So, how could she come at me, or judge me about the lack of time me and Staten spent together. My main focus was a healthy baby. Even if we didn't spend time my whole pregnancy, I knew he would still be a good damn father to our child, so nothing else mattered.

"Well, stop worrying about me. I'm not your child and I can handle myself... okay?"

She put her hands up in the air and cut her eyes at me. "Fine. All I'm trying to do is look out for you."

"And I appreciate that, but you have to stop trying to run my life. I know what works for me and my life. What works for you, won't work for me and vice versa," I told her.

"Whatever."

"Don't get an attitude about it now," I rolled my eyes. "What is new with you?"

"Moving."

"Huh?"

"I think I want to move out of Staten Island. The city or something. Trac doesn't want me out here anymore and wants me safe."

"So because Trac says it, you want to do it?"

"With him getting deeper in the streets, he wants to make sure that I'm safe at all times," I couldn't believe this was coming out of her mouth. Mariah could make a shot from miles away and had grown men piss their pants. This pampered wife role she played pissed me off because I knew she was more than this.

"Doesn't he know that you could protect yourself? We've been training since we were kids, you could protect yourself better than he could protect you."

"What if I'm tired of protecting myself? It feels nice having a man give a damn about you. Mami wanted us to be independent and I know how to be, but I like to feel protected too."

"Mami wanted a lot of things for us and we're doing the opposite."

Mariah sighed. "I love Mami, I really do, but she wanted this life. We didn't ask to miss out on our childhood to train. I want to be a wife, mother and focus on making my house a home for me and my man. Look at you, you're having a baby. I know you didn't think that would happen, but you're the happiest that I've seen you because of it."

She was right. A baby seemed like it was the end of the world at first, and now I couldn't see myself not being pregnant. I had so many plans for my baby that it kept me up at night. I wanted my child to have a childhood. Shit, I didn't even want my kid involved with this life. Me and its father was in the streets, so they needed to go to college and make me proud. I would raise my kid the opposite of me and I couldn't wait to do it. If my mother was around, it would be awesome because I would love for her to get to know her grandchild. If not, I know where we stand. I knew one thing, the position she put me in, I would never do to my child – ever.

"In the end, she needs to realize that it's about what makes us happy. How come daddy can be happy and support us, but she can't?"

"Because this isn't what she wanted for us. What she wants has to be done the way she wants it done. She can't see that I'm happy with Trac, or you're happily pregnant. All she sees is that we betrayed her by doing the opposite."

"What if Papi acted the same way she did when Daddy met him for the first time? She tends to forget she was on the other side too at one time."

"Papi is in Italy, and she doesn't tell him everything when he does call. I'm tired of living life for her, so I'm doing whatever I want to do," Mariah scoffed.

I hated how she chose to live her life, yet I had no other choice than to respect her. She wanted to live the way she wanted because it made her happy. Seeing how much Trac loved my sister, made me happy for her. She had found someone who loved her and wanted to spend their life with her. The added bonus was that he never backed down to my mother and made it his business to talk to my father man to man. How could you hate a man like that? Plain and simple; you couldn't.

I leaned up on the couch and grabbed my grape soda. It was the one thing I had been craving. Mariah claimed I was too early on for cravings, but all I wanted was a damn grape soda on ice. When I came over, I had brought a three-liter soda and my own bag of ice. I couldn't run the risk that she didn't have any ice or her fridge wasn't producing any. I needed to know that I had both of the things I wanted.

"I want a baby," she randomly blurted.

"Why? Because I have one?"

"I had a miscarriage a few months ago. Trac told me he

wants to wait to try again." Mariah never got into the deep logistics of she and Trac's business. I never knew she had a miscarriage and probably wouldn't have if she never told me. They were like Beyoncé and Jay-Z, they told you what they wanted you to know.

"I'm sorry, Riah. You should have told me."

"I didn't want to tell anyone. It was hard enough and I felt like such a failure for losing the baby. It's hard to explain," she sighed.

"It isn't your fault. You can't help what your body does," I told her. "I'm sorry I didn't notice or wasn't there for you. I know I can be selfish and end up wrapped into my own life."

"You were there when it mattered. It mattered even more because you were there for me and didn't know why I needed you."

"I'll always show up for you. If Trac isn't ready, let him become ready. You both have the rest of your lives to be together and make babies. Don't rush it, enjoy your man," I winked.

"Says the pregnant bitch."

"Look, I didn't plan on losing my virginity and then getting pregnant. Things happened and now I'm sitting here with a baby in my stomach."

"I'm really happy for you, Maliah. I can't wait to be an auntie and help you with everything," she smiled. I could tell she was excited for me. Even if she didn't agree on me and Staten's situation, my sister would always ride for me, no matter what.

"I know you are. I'm happy that you found Trac. Yeah, I give him shit, but I love how much he loves and respects you. If he wants you to move to protect you, then I support it."

"Girl, he was buying me a penthouse in the city, I was going with or without your blessing." We both fell out laughing because it was true. Hell, if someone offered me that, I would take it too.

You home?

Nah.

I'm heading to your crib. I smiled when I saw his message and started gathering my things. The fact that this was the first time I would be seeing him in a few weeks, made me smile. I wanted to just smell him and see his face.

"Where the hell you going?" Mariah saw me gathering my things up and slipping my feet into my sneakers.

"I gotta meet someone about something. If I don't, I'll hear Mami's mouth."

"I hear you. Call me when you get home," she got up and hugged me. We hugged and I was off to head to my house.

When I arrived at my house, Staten was waiting in the driveway. I pulled behind him and got out of the car. When he saw me, he got out of the car and came over to hug me. We hugged for a minute before we pulled apart and went into the house. I put my purse on the foyer table and went to the fridge to pour me some water. I had drank so much soda at Mariah's house, I knew I needed some water to cut the sugar down.

"I've missed you," he was the first to speak.

"I missed you too."

"You don't act like it," he countered.

"How do you want me to act?"

"Like you've missed me."

I rolled my eyes. "I can say the same thing. For someone who claims they missed me, hasn't called or came by to see me."

He leaned onto the wall and stared at me. "I been wrapped up in some shit and couldn't get away. I'm here now, what's up?"

I walked over to him and stared up at him. "Nothing, except air and opportunity," I cocked my head to the side.

He invaded the small space between the both of us and

looked at me through narrowed eyes. I watched as he bent down and placed small, yet wet kisses on my collar bone. The action alone sent chills through my soul, as I held onto his arm to keep myself from melting right there on the kitchen floor. A small moan escaped my lips as his lips kissed up and down my neck, leaving wet marks.

"Staten, you're not playing fair," I moaned out, as he held onto my waist and backed me up against the counter.

"How so?" he continued to suck on my neck as he pulled my shirt up over my head. That was the only time he took a break from the kisses. I stood in front of him with my bra and a pair of jeans on.

"You know how much I've missed you and you're using your lips to make me give in to you," I continued.

"Your body is giving in to my command, don't blame me," he lifted me up on the counter and tossed my sneakers off and slid my pants off my bottom. When I felt his hands on my lace panties, I knew there would be a puddle if he chose to lift me up from this counter. It was something about Staten that drove me crazy and made me want to give him my all. Staten Davis had that hold over me and I wasn't ashamed to say it or scream it to the world.

"I want to feel you inside of me. I missed your dick so much," I moaned out as his thumb massaged my kitty. I felt like my shit was hot and purring that's how turned on I was. All he had to do is blow on my pussy and I'd take a gun and shoot whoever he wanted me to shoot.

"Damn, you begging for the dick now? I gotta stay away more often," he smirked.

"Noooo, I don't want to be apart from you anymore," I wrapped my legs around his waist and hoisted myself up on him. I reached down and directed his dick inside of me and my eyes bulged at him pushing himself further and further inside of me.

Staten laid me down onto the counter and continued to push himself inside of me. At one point, I didn't think he would run out of dick to give. I leaned my head back as he pulled out and shoved himself inside of me quickly. I screamed out in pleasure as I scratched his chest. His veins were bulging on that beautiful piece of machinery he liked to refer to as a dick. I could feel his shit pulsating inside of me. Staten lifted one of my legs and continued to assault my cat like he had not one care in the world. I screamed, grabbed the counter and even knocked down the fruit basket. If my neighbors were home, I'm sure they thought I was in here about to be murdered. In fact, I was, he was murdering the hell out of this pussy, and I enjoyed him doing so. He pushed both my legs to the side and slid inside and then out before taking it out and tapping it right on my pussy. He did it a few times and I felt like I was about to explode. Staten wasn't doing small taps; he had enough dick to hold in his hand and slap right onto my pussy. The smirk he kept giving me turned me on just as much as slapping his shit right onto my pussy did.

"Put it inside of me, Staten!" I screamed out.

"Do it for me," he put his hands behind his head and stood there. In one swift movement, I lifted myself up, grabbed hold of his dick and inserted it inside of me.

"Fuck me, please, I'm tired of begging."

"That's all you had to say," he leaned over the counter and gave me the business. I came six times, and he hadn't come even once. The way he flipped me over and did me on that counter told me he hadn't had sex in a while. This was the act of someone who was not only frustrated, but not needed it more than anything. When he finally did come, he carried me into my room where we continued what we had started in the kitchen. I didn't care, long as I had him under my roof. I missed the time we used to spend, so I was going to make up for lost time.

8

Liberty

It had been a month since I had been in this rehab. Even though it wasn't nearly as expensive as the one that Staten paid for, I liked this one better. After the month, I was able to go out for day passes, which I loved. Everything was hard as hell the first month because I literally had to detox my whole body again. Chance was excited that I was getting better again. I hated having to explain to him that mommy was sick again. I cried for three hours after our conversation because I let him down. After talking with Ty, I found my *why* and it was Chance. He already had to live with the fact that he didn't see me often, but then I was also addicted to drugs. Chance didn't ask to be here, and he didn't ask to have a fuck up as a mother. He was my reason. I was also tired of disappointing my family. My mother called me two weeks into being here, and she told me I needed to get myself together. I knew it was true but hearing her tell me that she was disappointed in me and that I needed to change hit hard for me.

Ty had been my rock through this entire thing. He came up on visitation days and on my day passes, he took me out and we had so much fun. We ate at a nice restaurant, or we would just ride the Staten Island Ferry and talk. It came so easy when it came to Ty. He would ask me how I was doing, then he would leave it alone. He didn't hound me to continue to talk about it like Staten did. I knew Staten cared, but he made me feel like I was with a sober coach and that's not what I needed. I had to be the one who wanted to change. He couldn't be the reason I changed, or else it would never work. Sooner than later, I would sit down and chat with Staten. We were good before my truth was revealed. Life and other things became too much for our relationship and that was alright. It was fine for people to grow apart. Still, I missed the friend in him and wanted that back more than anything.

"You know you make me happy, right?" Ty told me. We were sitting outside the rehab at the tables. I was coloring in an adult that Ty had gifted me. I was nearly done with the book because it was all I did in my spare time.

"I know, you've told me," I looked up at him briefly, before looking back down at my coloring book. He made me happy too.

"Nah, I don't think you know how much you mean to me."

"Why you saying all of this?" I closed my book and paid closer attention to him. Where was all of this coming from?

"I'm saying. I want you to know how much you mean to me, Liberty. No other woman has made me feel the way you do. I just want to protect the shit out of you," he sighed and rubbed the side of my face.

"You mean a lot to me too. I love how you accept me and don't pass judgement on me. Even when you don't have to, you're up here to visit me on visitation days."

I took a sip of my soda and smiled when he looked at me. "I want you to marry me."

I choked on my soda and looked at him through wide eyes, as I continued to choke. "M... marry you?"

"Yeah, I'm dead ass serious. What's stopping us from taking that step? I want to share everything I have with you. I'm looking for a wife, and I told you that from day one."

"You have, but wife... that's a big step. I'm not wifey material, and I don't think I ever will be."

"Being yourself is all that I need, Liberty. I don't need a perfect wife, I just need a real one, and you're real. You've been through shit like me and you understand me."

"Um... uh... shit, you caught me off guard," I giggled because for once in my life, I was at a loss for words.

"That's new," he joked and I hit him. "I didn't plan this when I got up this morning. This shit just feels right, so who says you need years under your belt to decide if someone is right to propose to? I know this is right when I see your face."

My hands shook as he grabbed them and placed a kiss on top of them. "You're fucking crazy!" I laughed.

"Crazy for your ass," he replied. "Will you do me the honors and become my wife?" he asked once more and the impulsive side of me told me to jump at this. What did I have to lose?

"Yes, I'll be your wife," I giggled and hugged him. We kissed and hugged as I stared at my future husband.

I made this decision on a clear head, not one that was clouded by drugs. "You just made me happy as shit today. I want you to meet my family and all that shit when you get out of here."

"I guess you need to meet mine too," I chuckled, thinking about how crazy it would sound when I told Freedom that I was getting married.

"And, when you get out, I want you to move into my condo with me. I want to make this real, ma. You hear me?"

"I hear you, babe. I'll move in, but I need to keep my place because it's close to my job," It was a miracle that I still had a damn job.

"Nah, quit that shit. You're going to be my wife and I want to spoil you."

All of that sounded good, but I hadn't told him about Chance. "I have a son. He has down syndrome," I revealed. Nothing changed, his face remained the same.

"So, what you saying is I'll have a step-son?"

I nodded my head.

"Ma, you could tell me that you have a sheep with three heads and I'll still love the shit out of you. I want to meet him."

"You will. Soon," I promised.

We hugged and I caressed his face. Ty made me happy. I loved being around him, and when I wasn't around him, I couldn't wait until the next time we could be together. It didn't matter that we had only been talking for a short while, the chemistry that we had was like no other. I had done much crazier shit than marrying someone I hadn't been with for long, so I was screaming yolo the entire time. My fear was how Freedom was going to react. I was tired of her thinking that she was my boss, because she wasn't. I knew I had made stupid decisions in the past, but I was old enough to dictate what went on in my own life. Free would do everything in her power to try and end things between me and Ty. The reason I kept him quiet was because my fear on how my family would react. They felt like I should have been trying to get with Staten and that wasn't what my heart wanted. I loved Staten, still, I knew that it wouldn't work out with us. He was scared. When I said scared, I knew he wasn't scared to love me, but he was scared to do anything with me. He worried about my sobriety more than I did.

We would also argue and rather than endure that again, it was best that he lived his life and I lived mine. In the future, if it was meant to be, we would come together and be friends again. Anything outside of being friends would never last. I was too strong willed for Staten, and he liked girls that allowed him to pick and choose how he wanted things to be. At first, he acted like he was alright with it, then as time went on, he realized that it wasn't what he was used to, and he couldn't handle me. Time would only tell if Ty could handle my smart-ass mouth. So far, he seemed to be fine with it. I refused to change for a nigga. I understood submitting for a man, but I wasn't about to be out here being a fool for a man. I had done that once when I was younger and I refused to do it as an grown ass woman.

"What's on your mind?" I asked Ty. He was in his phone, but I remained on his lap. If it was one thing I could change, it was the fact that he always had that damn phone glued to his hands.

"I need to find you a ring. Can't have my fiancée walking around with a bare finger," he kissed my hand and looked me in the eyes.

"Do you think you'll always have your phone glued to your hands? I mean, once we're married and stuff?" I wondered.

I loved a man that worked and earned his money. Ty had many nice things and I could tell it was because he worked hard for it. Still, I didn't want to be a wife that got whatever she wanted, but the one thing I wanted was my husband and I couldn't have him.

He put his phone down and looked at me. "I'm not going to lie and say that I won't be working, but I will promise to be better as your husband and make time for you."

"Only if you promise," I batted my eyelashes.

"I promise. I want to give you the world and that's going to take money. I'm not going to sit here and sell you a dream. I may miss some things because I have to travel, but once you start having our babies, I'll stop traveling as much to be there for you.

"Babies?" I choked out.

I would have been a fool to think he didn't want children, still, I wasn't thinking about babies anytime soon. I didn't even want any more children. Having Chance alone was traumatic enough for me not to ever have any more children. Ty looked at me with so much love in his eyes and I couldn't bring myself to tell him that I didn't want any more kids. It was something I would have to tell him. It didn't have to be right now.

"Hell yeah. I want three kids, all boys."

"You know you can't pick the gender, right?"

"Ma, I got enough money to pick out three boys. We don't have to worry about that right now," he kissed me on the lips. "Whenever that time comes, we'll discuss that."

"Okay," I muttered.

There was no need to get in my feelings about something that wasn't happening right away. I had time to tell him I didn't want children. Right now, I needed to focus on telling my sisters that I was getting married. I was mentally preparing myself to hear Free's mouth about me marrying a stranger. For once, I was doing something that I wanted to do. The hard part would be trying to get Justice up here because she was still not talking to me.

Can you and Justice come visit me? I have to tell you both something. I sent Free a text message while Ty was on the phone.

Of course. Something wrong?

Just need to see you both and talk.

I'll come after I finish at the office. Let me call Jus and see if she's free too.

K.

I put my phone away and watched as Ty paced the garden, giving orders out. He put his phone back into his pocket and came over to me. "Babe, I gotta go."

"I know, work calls," I replied and stood up while gathering my coloring book and pencils. "Drive safe, please."

He hugged me and kissed me on the lips. "I will. Call you tonight."

"K," I replied and walked back to the building, while he walked through the gates to the parking lot. I stood outside the door and watched his yellow Lamborghini whip out the parking lot.

He beeped his horn when he got onto the street and I waved before going into the building. When I walked in, my therapist was just coming in to start her shift. "Hey Liberty!"

"Hi, Miranda," I smiled and continued to go upstairs to my room.

This center wasn't nearly as glamorous as the one that Staten paid for, but the help was different. I could relate to the people in group circle more than the other ones. In the other rehab, they were stars, rich and had money to spend on treatments for the rest of their lives. Plus, their family wasn't disappointed because they had money. I wiped my savings out and was literally living on the small amount of money that I had under my couch. Having a coke habit was expensive, especially when you did it as frequently as I did. Free was paying my rent because I had no more paid time at work. I laid across the bed and looked at the ceiling before my eyes grew heavy and eventually, I was fast asleep.

"Liberty?" I heard my name being called.

I stirred from my sleep and looked at the clock. "Yeah?"

"You have visitors downstairs," the nurse told me.

"Thank you. Let me fix myself and I'll be down there," I promised and went to the bathroom. I washed my face, put some lip gloss on and fix my messy bun into a neat one.

Why was I so nervous to tell them? It was my life and I was grown, right? I could do whatever I wanted, so they couldn't tell me that I could not marry Ty. What if they didn't like him and then I married him? So many questions were swirling around my mind and I didn't know what to say or do. How do I start a conversation that I'm getting married when they didn't even know I was dating? All these thoughts continued to attack my mind when I got downstairs. I entered the visitation room and spotted Free and Justice sitting at a table near the window. I smiled as I headed over to them. Free stood up and hugged me.

"Your skin looks so good and clear," she complimented.

"Thanks," I sat down when I realized that Justice wasn't going to stand up. "Thanks for coming, Justice."

"Sure," she replied, being short.

"What's going on? You had me worried with that text message?" Free jumped right into the conversation.

"How's Ghost and Samoor?"

"Ghost is doing good and Samoor's heart hasn't declined, so we're good. Now, tell me what is going on that I had to drive here to see you."

I sighed and then looked at both of them. "I'm getting married," I revealed.

Justice had been so busy texting on her phone, but when I mentioned I was getting married, she looked up at me. "Married?" she blurted. "To who?"

"I've been dating a guy and he makes me happy. It hasn't been that long, but he asked me to marry him and I told him yes."

"Does he know you do drugs, have a son and come with a lifelong addiction?" Justice beat Free to the punch.

"He knows all of that. I made sure to tell him all of that."

Free shook her head. "Married, Liberty? You're determined to send me to an early grave. Why can't you just be with him, why do you have to marry him?" she wondered.

"Because he asked me to marry him. I love him," I admitted.

"Love him?" Justice spat. "You need to fall in love with yourself first before trying to marry a nigga. Focus on you."

"I could have said the same thing about you jumping from your ex right to Priest, but I supported your ass. I'm not asking for you both to try and piece together what I'm doing. All I'm asking is for you both to support me, even if you don't agree."

"It's your life. I don't give a damn what you do with it." Justice stood up. "Oh, and I jumped to Priest because he showed me love. You've been high jumping from nigga to nigga, without being worried about your son. The only man you should be worried about is your son; Chance."

"When I get on my feet, I'm going to move him back to the city."

Justice cackled so loud that a few people surrounding us turned to look our way. "If you want to be a good mother, leave Chance where he is. Lord knows he can't afford to find you sprawled on the couch unconscious too," she snapped. "Free, I'll call you later. Thank God I borrowed Staten's car," she mumbled on her way out.

Justice hated me and there was nothing I could do that would change the way she felt. I could hear the hate and hurt drip off her tongue when she spoke to me. Even when she looked at me, it wasn't the same as before. She looked disgusted and upset that she even had to be in my presence.

"She'll come around. Justice is dealing with so much that I can't even get through to her sometimes," Free tried to soften the blow that Justice had threw.

"She hates me, and I know it's my fault."

"Justice doesn't hate you. She's hurt and still dealing with finding you unconscious. That's a lot for someone to deal with, so give her a break."

"I am."

"You're not. The way you just tried to diss her for moving on to be with Priest wasn't you giving her a break. She just had her daughter months early, Priest missed the birth because he was cheating and if that wasn't enough, she found you damn near dead. She has a lot going on and is probably trying to sort things out. Be easy on her."

"Alright," I agreed.

"I love you and I'm proud of you. You took that first step without any of us forcing you. So, for that, I'm so proud of you," she told me and rubbed my hand. "I want to meet this fiancé of yours."

"Whenever you want."

"Okay. Schedule something for tomorrow. I'll get out the office early."

"K."

"Can you do me a favor?"

"Yeah."

"Can you ask Staten to come up here? The last time we were together it didn't end right, and I want to apologize to him. More than anyone, he has wanted me to get clean and I just want him to see that I'm clean and that I'm going to do it for real this time."

"I can call him and tell him. Being completely honest, I thought you and Staten would be getting married."

"Once upon a time ago, I thought the same," I admitted. "I know he'll be hesitant since I barked his head off last time, but can you please tell him to come."

"Staten does what he wants, but I'll do my best to convince him to come."

"Thank you."

"Anytime." We sat chatting for a minute before visitation hours were over. I wished like hell I was leaving out with my sister. Being in this place was what was best for me, but sometimes I wished that I could walk out those doors and live a regular life. One day... One day.

9

_____

Staten
I'm way too good at goodbyes – Sam Smith

It took me a week to come up to this rehab center to visit Liberty. When Free told me that she wanted to see me, I was hesitant. Since she barked on me the last time, I was letting her live her life the way she wanted. Shit, I had a bunch of other shit going on in my own life, so if she wanted me out, I was giving her the space she wanted. I was surprised when Free told me that she decided to admit herself into rehab. It took a lot for her to do something like that, so the least I could do was come up to visit her. I turned my car off and walked through the gravel parking lot to the front door. This place was nothing like the place I had paid for before. Liberty couldn't afford that place, so I understood why she chose this place. When I walked through the door, I signed my name and was shown to the visitation room. I decided to sit outside since it was a nice day.

Being inside this place had me feeling like I was visiting a homie on lock down.

"Hey, you," I heard from behind me.

I turned around and Liberty was standing there wearing a green maxi dress that fell down to the floor. Her hair was curled, and a piece was pinned back to keep from falling in her face. She didn't have a lick of make-up on. That was when I found her to be the most beautiful anyway.

"What's good?" I walked over to her and hugged her. She smelled like French vanilla and lilacs. My arms swallowed her whole frame in our embrace.

"I'm just hanging," she smiled. "Sit," she pointed to the picnic table behind us.

I took a seat and stared into her face. "You look good, Lib."

She messed with a piece of hair, and that's when I noticed a big ass rock sitting on her ring finger. Liberty noticed when I saw it and quickly put her hand down. "Thank you," she stammered.

"What's the ring about?"

She looked away, then looked back. Our eyes connected and I refused to let her look away again. "I'm engaged, Staten."

"Engaged? Stop fronting."

Her face remained serious. Liberty was too silly to hold this in, if she was joking. "I'm serious. I got engaged a week ago."

The shit hit me like a sack of bricks. I knew we weren't in a good place, yet I thought I always had time to get my girl back. With her being engaged, there was no way I would be able to get my girl back.

"Who is this nigga?"

"Nobody that you know," she vaguely replied. "I didn't ask you to come here for that."

"So why the fuck did you ask me to come? That big ass ring would have been hard to fucking miss."

"I didn't even know he was going to get me a ring until he popped up with the ring last week. I don't want to hurt you."

"Nah, why would that hurt me?" I acted like that shit was water and rolled off me. On the inside, my heart was beating and the thought of me and Liberty ever being together seemed to be fading more and more.

"Good. I'm glad you're not hurt. I wanted to apologize for the last time we had saw each other. You've always been the one to help me, despite everything. I always push and fight with you, but you never had let me down when it came to helping me," she pulled a envelope from under the table. "Here's a check for the cost of the rehab that you paid for. I wasted your time and money and I'm sorry for that."

"How'd you get this money?"

"My fianc—"

"I'll slap the shit out of you. Don't you ever hand me the next nigga's money. I did that shit because I cared for you, not because I wanted my money back."

She removed the envelope and stared at me before she spoke. "What is it that you want from me?"

"Liberty, all I have ever wanted was just you. I wanted you and only you, but me wanting you was never enough for you. You fought me every step of the way until eventually you didn't want this anymore."

Your mom isn't answering the phone. I need her to watch Satin. I have to fly to Miami, cousin graduation, I saw Chanel's text pop up on the screen.

Chanel was starting to remind me of Shakira's ass. When my moms wanted the baby, she wanted to act like she was busy, but the moment she had to do something it was alright for my mom to take the baby.

"We're not good for each other. Too much has happened, and I can admit the reason so much has happened was because of me. You didn't deserve the shit I put you through."

"And the next nigga does? You put me through shit, but then go and love the next nigga? Why does he get the version of you that I've been begging for?"

Helloooooooooooo.

I sighed looking at another text message that Chanel had sent.

"This shit will follow me for the rest of my life, so I disagree with him getting the best version of me. I just want you to be happy and find someone who loves as hard as you," her voice cracked.

"Nah, don't do that crying shit," I told her and looked away.

"I can't help it, Staten. I love you and don't want you to hurt."

"If you love me, give that man his ring back and be with me. That's what someone who loves me would do."

"I can't...."

"Bet. I wish you the best, Liberty. I really do. I want you to find happiness within yourself and not another situation. You already know that I'm a phone call away if you need me," I stood up and walked over to her side. I bent down and kissed her forehead. "Keep your head up, you got this."

She was crying and I didn't want to stay and see her hurting. I couldn't change her mind and that big ass ring on her finger already told me that she made her decision. I had never wanted to be with a woman so bad in my entire life. Yet, I had to realize that I couldn't have something that didn't want me back. If me and Liberty was meant to be, then we would be together. At the end of the day, I just wanted her clean and happy so she could be a good mother to Chance. He didn't deserve any of the shit that she was putting him through when she checked into these rehabs. He was the only person that mattered, and I prayed that she allowed herself to get the help she needed and didn't use this new nigga as a crutch.

I guess Chanel got tired of texting and before I knew it, she was calling me. When I got into my car, I decided to call her back. She didn't let the phone ring before she was on the phone.

"Shaliq, why do I have to text and call like a mad woman?"

"You acting like I don't be busy. I got your message and I'm on my way to pick her up," I told her and ended the call.

I would be fronting if I lied and said I didn't miss when me and Chanel were just friends. I missed us having conversations and not doing this arguing shit. All we did was argue about shit that I couldn't control. She wanted me to stop working so much, I tried to dial back the hours, then when I did, she complained that she felt smothered and I treated her like she didn't know how to take care of Satin. Nothing was ever good enough for her and I was tired as fuck trying to please her. Her new issue was that she wanted a new place because she was tired of staying with her parents. What confused the shit out of me was that she had her own place and was choosing to stay with her parents, in her old bedroom.

When I offered to move her, she refused. Now, she refused to move unless it was the condos that cost in the millions. I understood my daughter needed to have a nice place to lay her head down, yet she didn't have to live in no damn million-dollar condo. Shit, she wouldn't know the damn difference. Chanel just wanted to show off and let everyone know that she had a baby daddy that made shit happen. I didn't understand why she felt the need to please all her friends, who had broke ass baby daddies. I could buy her a toy stroller and it would still be more than any of their baby daddies ever provided.

On my way to Chanel's parents' house, I called my mother. Me and Satin would be good, but when I had to head out, I needed my mother to watch her while I was gone. Chanel acted like I didn't know how to raise my own daughter. If she stopped always being a helicopter parent, then I would have learned half the shit I needed to learn about Satin already. It wasn't only her; it was her parents too.

"Hey baby boy!" my mother answered the phone. I needed to check in more with my old lady.

"What's up, mama? How you?"

"I'm good. Me and Mirror just got back from the nail shop."

"Tell Mir, I said what's up?"

"Miss you, Staten!" I heard Mirror yell through the phone. It had been a minute since I kicked it with baby sis. Mirror lived her life and didn't like to involve anyone into it. Shit, she could be married with kids and none of us would know because she kept that shit secret.

"We gotta get up," I promised her.

"Soon," she replied.

"What's going on with you? You don't ever call," my mama already was hip to my bullshit. "You okay, right?"

"I'm good, mama. Chanel is going out of town for a few days and I'm gonna have Satin. When I'm working through the day, you mind keeping an eye on her?"

"Now you know I don't. Bring her by whenever. I want to spend as much time as I can before her mama comes back."

"I got you," I told her and ended the call just as I pulled up to her parent's house.

Outside, I sent her a text message. Since Satin's birth, I didn't fuck with her parents and it would always be like that.

Chanel came out the door, struggling with all Satin's stuff. I got out the car and helped her down the stairs. "I typed out a list for your mother to follow."

"I'm going to be caring for her. Why would I drop her off to my mother when she's my daughter?"

"Oh, so you're going to be baby-sitting. Well, follow the list. I spent two hours on it."

"Chanel, no grown man baby sits his kids. The fuck you think this is?"

"Anyway, I'll be back in four days. My cousin graduates, so I'm going for that and to spend time out there. I need a getaway. She has enough pumped milk packed. If she needs more, my dad is staying, so call him and he'll drop some more from the freezer off to you."

"Ight."

"Let me go get her. Put the adapter into the car," she told me as she jogged back up the steps.

Chanel wasn't like those celebrities on Instagram; models who bragged about their snapback. Satin was two months old and she still had about sixty pounds on her. I liked that shit because it showed me that she real. A bitch who was skinny a week after giving birth was weird to me. I wanted to see you thick and still working that shit off. Carrying a baby and then delivering one wasn't no easy shit, so getting the weight off wasn't either. I put the adapter into the car and leaned on my car while waiting for her to return with the baby. When she came down, I gently grabbed my daughter and kissed her on the lips. I missed her little rubber like lips.

"Damn, she looking more and more like you," I kissed her again on the lips and placed her into the car seat.

"Cause I did that," she bragged. "She's just beautiful like her mama," she handed me a mirror that allowed me to see her when I was driving.

"I have some say in it too. Cause it was my soldiers that got her here," I winked.

"Whatever. You better take care of my baby."

"She's mine too. I got her. Relax," I told her and checked on a sleeping Satin once more before getting into the car. "Text me when you land."

"I will. You better follow those instructions," she made sure to mention again.

I pulled off and headed home. After sitting down with Liberty earlier, I wasn't in the mood to do shit else, except lay-up and chill with my baby girl. My phone rang and I thought it was Chanel, but it was Maliah. I pressed the button and her voice came through the phone.

"Do you wanna know what we're having?" she asked.

"How do you know?"

"My doctor was able to see, and she told me," she sounded mad excited. Her excitement made me excited.

"Tell me," I was excited to know what we would be having. Maliah had been real low-key with her pregnancy. She didn't complain or make excuses like Chanel's ass did. She barely mentioned the baby unless I did. If she was this laid back and cool, parenting with her would be a breeze.

"We're having a little boy," she screamed through the phone.

"Word! Yes, I got my little boy!" I hollered back. Satin screamed out and then stuck her hand into her mouth to soothe herself.

"I'm so happy. I don't think I could have done a girl... you have your daughter?"

"Man, I can't do two daughters. I'm mad excited. Thank you. Yeah, Chanel going out of town."

"No, thank you. You could have told me to get rid of it, and wanted no parts, but you've been here for me as much as time allows," she said. "And, I'll link with you later. Enjoy time with the little one."

"Nah, come by my crib."

"Okay," she agreed.

We ended the call and I drove to the supermarket and grabbed a cake. I had the baker scribble some words on it and then went to the party aisle. By the time I got to the crib, I was wondering how all mothers did this shit. All I did was grab three items and Satin cut up the entire time. She shitted, so I had to go into the men's bathroom and change her. Why the hell didn't they have changing tables in the men's bathroom? By the time I made it to pay and got into the car I needed a damn nap before I could head home. Then, once we got into the house, she screamed so damn loud I'm sure the neighbors thought I was trying to kill her. I followed the directions that Chanel sent, and she was calm and eating within three minutes. After I burped her, I took her into the nursery I had done for her and laid her down. She looked at me for a few before her eyes started to flutter open and close. Eventually, she lost the fight and went to sleep.

While she was sleep, I blew up balloons and sat out the cake. This was Maliah's first child and her mother already wasn't excited or wanted to be apart, so as her baby's father, I had to make it special for her. Women always threw those gender reveal shits, and since she didn't do it, she deserved some kind of celebration. Even if it was something small, she deserved to be celebrating because she was welcoming life into this world. By the time I set everything up, I had to go and feed Satin and change her into pajamas. By that time, I was tired and climbed on the couch to rest my eyes. I jumped out of my sleep when I heard someone banging on the front door. The drool was on my faux fur pillows and shit. I crept to the front door and when I saw Maliah, I let her in.

"I thought you hadn't got here yet. It doesn't help that the whole house is dark, and you always park in the garage," she laughed as she hugged me. "I had to check on a few things before coming over here."

"You're good. Satin had my ass knocked out."

"Hard, huh?"

"Hell yeah. I don't know how I'm going to juggle two," I walked into the kitchen. My back was turned, but I heard her gasps.

"You didn't have to do this, Staten." When I turned around, her hands were to her mouth and she had a shocked expression on her face. "You're about to make me cry," her voice cracked.

"Don't get all emotional on me," I laughed.

"I can't help it. You didn't have to do this, but you did and it means a lot to me. I'm really lucky that I have you to go through this with."

"Like I told you, I got you and our son," I rubbed her stomach. Maliah had a damn six pack at one time, and now it was more like a pudge.

"I'm really excited to have this baby. I can't wait until he comes because then I can stop being so damn emotional."

"Don't rush him. He's coming," I hugged her again and then went to cut her a piece of cake. The way she eyeing the cake, I knew she would want a piece.

"I want a big piece too."

"How's your mother been? You spoke to her?"

"When it comes to business, yeah. Other than that, I don't hear from her. She doesn't want to know anything about the baby."

"She'll come around."

"You know my mom. She's not going to come around. Honestly, I don't care because it feels good doing something that I want to do."

"I need to go holla at her sometime soon."

"Why?"

"I don't want my son being rejected by his grandmother. As much as she doesn't like the situation, she can't control the shit and need to just accept it like everyone else."

"Have you told your mother?"

"Nah. I told Priest and Ghost."

She sat down at the counter and dug into the cake. "And what did they have to say?"

"Shit, they were shocked and told me I was crazy as fuck."

"For fucking one of Messiah's daughters, right?"

"Yeah. Everyone knows your mother doesn't play when it comes to the both of you. I didn't plan for any of this to happen, but it did. What does she want me to do? Act like a deadbeat and not acknowledge that the baby is mine?"

"My mom is weird. As much as I want her support, I don't need it. Long as I keep up with the business side of things, she's good."

"Business is business when it comes to your mother," I sighed.

My mother needed to know what was going on and about Maliah having my baby. I couldn't keep this a secret anymore. Shit, I needed to tell Chanel. That would be a whole other problem. My mother loved her grandchildren, so she would be excited for the new baby. Chanel on the other hand, she would be pissed because she was ready to work on baby two and I had been ignoring her ass about it. It wasn't like I did this shit on purpose. After my son was born, I needed to start wrapping my shit up. I couldn't be having all these damn kids, and it didn't matter if I could afford them either.

SINCE CHANEL GAVE me enough time with Satin, I spent two days in the crib with her. We watched movies, ate and I had to change her diapers a shit load of times. She had a big blow out and got shit all over my damn bed. The time was needed. I had Liberty on my mind, and I needed to distance myself from everyone for a minute. Although two days wasn't enough time to deal with everything, money was calling, and I had to get to making it. When Ghost stepped down, it left everything up to me, so two days away was like a month off. I carried Satin into my mother's house. It never failed, she always had something cooking when I entered her door. I spent a lot of time at my mom's crib eating because I didn't know how to cook. The busier I got, the less time I had to just sit and chill with her while grubbing on her good ass food.

"Hey baby, you look tired," she observed, then her eyes

landed onto Satin, and suddenly I didn't matter as much anymore. "Look at this angel. You know I haven't seen her since she was in the hospital?"

"I'm sorry about that, mama. I really be on her ass, but she does what she wants."

She nodded her head as she looked into Satin's face. "Yeah, I know. You and your brother sure know how to pick them."

"Yeah, in Chanel's defense, she wasn't always like this."

"Just because you never saw it, doesn't mean she was never like this," she pointed her finger at me. "Go in that bathroom and brush your teeth. Man, your breath is killing me," she laughed.

"Do you know how long it takes to get a baby together?"

"Yep, I got three of them together."

I went into her linen closet and grabbed a fresh toothbrush. While she had Satin, I brushed my teeth and washed my face before going back into the kitchen where she was holding Satin. "Mama, I got another baby on the way," I blurted. There was no way to get around it. I had to just tell her.

"Dammit, Staten. I had the talk about protection with both you and your brother. Don't tell me it's by Chanel?"

"Maliah."

"Messiah's daughter?"

I nodded my head. "It just happened."

"And how does her mother feel about this?"

"She not happy. She'll live."

"Or maybe you won't live. What is wrong with you? That is reckless, Staten. That girl is too damn young to be a mother."

"Mama, she's twenty-one."

"And you're in your thirties. What do you have in common with a damn twenty-one-year-old?"

"A lot. I don't think about the age. She acts older than what she is. Ma, you know I hate those young acting chicks. It's something about Maliah that had me open and one thing led to another and now she's having my baby."

"How do you know the baby is yours?" she narrowed her eyes at me.

"Because I took her virginity."

"Good Jesus, Shaliq. Do you know what happens when you take a woman's virginity? You'll never get rid of her now," I knew that to be true. It was different when it came to Maliah. She wasn't clingy and she let me do my thing. When we would link together, she knew that was our time. When it was time to go our separate ways, she didn't give me an issue.

"She's not like that."

"Yeah, not yet... where do you see this going? Is this another baby mama, or do you see yourself being with this girl?"

I shrugged my shoulders. "I don't know, mama."

"You were so sure about Liberty, why is it so hard for you to know? Are you stringing this girl along?"

"I was wrong about Liberty, so now I'm being cautious about who I'm going to jump into a relationship with."

"Bullshit. Tell me right now do you see yourself being with Maliah and raising your child with her?"

I couldn't tell her that because I didn't. I loved Maliah, but I couldn't see myself being with her. I hated that I even got us this deep, but I couldn't be with her. The fact that Messiah would never approve didn't bother me, it was the fact that Maliah would go hard to avoid her mother to make our relationship work and I couldn't be the cause of that. Despite Messiah's fucked up parenting views, Maliah needed her mother. Maliah was very wise and mature for her age, which was why we connected on such a deep level. Still, she had so much life to experience and I couldn't take that from her. Right now, all she did was work and handle business for her mother, but what about when she woke up at thirty and realized she never got a chance to live and settled down with me? I didn't want her to resent me. Our son would always be good, and we would always co-parent, but I didn't see myself settling down and being with her. Especially when Liberty still had my heart.

"Nah," I admitted.

"Don't you think she should know? Stringing her along, and she's pregnant with your child creates problems."

"I hear you."

She sighed. "I hope so. I really hope you get your shit together. Having all these babies and not committing to these women is going to get you in a world of trouble. Especially, when you have to have those conversations with your kids."

I got up from the table and bent down to kiss Satin. "I definitely hear you, mama. Thank you for taking care of her for me."

"You know I love these kids. Go and handle your business, and please be safe."

"Always," I said and left out the door.

Everything my mother said was the truth. Eventually, I would have to explain to my kids why I never married their mamas. I had to shake back and get control of my life. Lately, it seemed like shit was going crazy. Even if my mama didn't think I was listening, I heard what she said and I had planned to make some changes with my life.

10

Justice

My life had been a shit show and I was trying hard to push through. However, when Yasmine came home two weeks ago, I felt like my life was finally trying to brighten up. She was able to come home and go straight into her own room in my apartment. This wasn't the vision I had for my life, yet I had to deal with it and take the cards life had dealt me. Priest was there to welcome Yasmine home. I didn't want him to know where I lived and tried hard to avoid it, but I couldn't take this moment away from him. As much as I couldn't stand him, my heart went out to him. He was dealing with Kiki suicide attempt, and then Love was staying out all times of night. His daughter coming home was the brightest thing to happen in his life, so I didn't want to deny him of that. As much as I loved the girls, I couldn't be there the way I wanted for them. They knew my number and knew if they needed me that I would come running. Right now, Yasmine and trying to get my life back in order was main priority.

This week the grand opening of my center was set to open. I had a whole bunch of parents that wanted to enroll their teens into our SAT prep programs. I even had parents of younger students who wanted them to be enrolled in tutoring, which was six days a week. My center and Yasmine were the only two things that I was excited about. Everything else in my life went straight to hell and I tried my best to ignore it all. Even with Yasmine being home, she still had a bunch of appointments and I made sure to take an Uber there to avoid having to sit in Priest's car and hear him apologize over and over again. His little bitch must have gotten my number and now she wouldn't stop calling me from different numbers. If that wasn't enough, she would send text messages with pictures of Priest sleeping beside her. He claimed it was old, but I didn't know what to believe. If he was still fucking around with her, then he needed to stop trying to get back with me. It was obvious that this bitch wanted him and wouldn't stop until he was hers – again.

"Are you ever going to make it right with Liberty?" Free asked, as she fed Samoor. She had come over to visit me and Yasmine. If I wasn't at the center, I was home with my daughter. I didn't even leave the house to food shop, I had that delivered to me.

"When she's clean for more than two months. I'm tired of getting my hopes up for her to fall back into the same pattern. I'm sick of it."

"She's due to get out of the rehab soon. Her fiancé had movers move things out of her apartment, she's giving it up." Free wanted me to care and I didn't. Whatever Liberty chose to do with her life, was her choice to make. If she truly found love, I was happy for her and prayed she didn't fuck it up.

"Didn't you say he had money?"

"Yeah. He's a cool dude. I could tell he's into Liberty more than she is into him," she put Samoor over her shoulder and gently burped him.

"How do you know?"

"I know her, and I know that he cares a great deal for her. I'm not saying Liberty doesn't care for him, but It's not as much as he cares for her."

"So, why do you think she wants to marry him? If Liberty doesn't want to do something, she doesn't do it, so why did she agree to marry him?"

Free shrugged her shoulders. "I have no clue. She's planning a whole wedding and has met his family."

"Met his family? This is serious."

"Uh huh. So, we need to support her. She seems to be happy and I don't want her to feel like we're not supporting her."

"Well, I don't support this. She needs to focus on herself before trying to get married."

"Yeah, well... it's not our place to say anything."

"What you mean? I found her damn near dead, I think I have a right to not support her," I rolled my eyes.

Finding my sister laid out on the couch and not knowing that she was alive or dead had me scared. It was something I couldn't stop thinking about. Liberty felt like that I should forget it and move on. It was hard to un-see something like that. Especially when it was your own sister. I couldn't stop thinking about how this could have gone wrong. Instead of visiting her in rehab, I could have been visiting her in the morgue. I wasn't ready to forgive her or have a conversation with her.

"I'm not saying you need to forget, but you do need to forgive her. Talk to her and see where her head is. I feel like she may get it right this time," Free tried to convince me.

"On my time. I'm not working on Liberty's time, just mine."

"That's fair."

"When do you and Ghost leave for vacation?"

She smiled. Free was so in love with Ghost. I knew with him having cancer it was hard, but she was managing to be there for him through it all. "Well, it turned out to be a family vacation. The kids are out for break, so we decided to bring them along with the nanny."

"I'm excited for you. You guys need this vacation more than anything," I smiled at her. With all that was going on, they needed some sun and quality time with their kids. "Did you guys decide where you're going?"

"We're going to Belize."

"What? I'm jealous. How do you think the kids will behave on a plane?"

She smiled. "We're taking the private jet. The kids will be able to have room and sleep when they want. I'm excited to just be getting out of the country and doing it with Gyson and the kids."

"Hopefully you get some dick too."

"Girl, I plan to. Gyson got some work done to his villa over the winter, so I'm excited to see what was done. He showed me pictures of the infinity pool he put in, and the kids can't wait to swim."

"I'm glad that everyone is excited. Me and Yasmine will be here watching re-runs and pumping milk."

"Did you doctor say you couldn't travel with her?"

"He says I can, I'm just not there yet. I still cry when I change her diaper because I don't want to hurt her. We'll eventually travel, just not yet."

"Do everything on your timing, mama," she offered me a smile. "The good thing is that she's home and not in the hospital anymore."

"That part."

"What's going on with you and Priest? I heard about Kiki, how is he doing with that?"

"Good. He got her into therapy, and she's being home-schooled. He handled it the best way he knew how. His problem is Love and her fast ass. She is following right after Kiss and he can't control her."

"Wow. And what about you and him?"

"What about us?"

"Do you think you'll ever forgive him and be with him again?"

"Do pigs fly?"

She giggled. "Seriously, Justice."

"I'm tired of niggas doing what they want, and I'm supposed to be alright with it, and accept it. Priest made his bed and now he has to lie in it. I don't know what the future holds, but he got a lot of ass kissing before I'll even consider it."

"I hear you... I know he does love you."

"He sure has a funny way of showing it. Right now, he needs to focus on his nieces and daughter. If we're gonna be together, only time will tell," I sighed. "On another note, I spoke to mommy."

"Oh yeah? I'm surprised."

"Me too. She called me and congratulated me on bringing Yasmine home. Told me she can't wait to come home so she can see her."

"Don't hold your breath. She hasn't even met Samoor."

"Do you think she's going through a midlife crisis or something?"

Free shook her head. "No, I think after daddy died that she had to be the strong parent and raise us. She had a job to do and to her, she feels like she has completed that job and is free to do what she wants."

"She kinda is."

"Yeah, but when does it become alright to forget about your

kids? My man is dying, and her grandson has a heart condition. You had your baby months early and she still hasn't come, shit, Liberty nearly died and all she did was call and tell her to get her shit together. Just because your kids are grown doesn't mean you stop being a parent."

"I agree with you," I could tell that this was something that bothered Freedom the most. My mother should have been here for us and she wasn't. Did it make me love her any less? No, having my sisters there for me was what mattered the most to me. My mom stopped talking to me after I chose to take my ex back after he nearly tried to kill us. I needed her the most then and she wasn't there because she allowed her personal feelings to get in the way of being there for me.

"Mom will come around when she wants. In the meantime, I'm excited to spending time with my family and actually enjoying ourselves. These past few months have been crazy and I think this trip is well needed."

"You definitely deserve this trip more than anyone."

"Wish you were going."

"Me too. We'll have another one real soon," I promised her.

You think having his baby means anything. Me and him have history. I was close with his big sister, you never even met her. I sighed and rolled my eyes at the text message from Lavern. It was getting so bad that I was able to set a time around when she would send a message or call from another number.

Free noticed my facial expression. "What's the matter?"

"Lavern. She texts and calls all the damn time about Priest. It's one thing that he cheated but having to be dragged into this shit with him is what irritates me."

"What does she want with you?"

"Your guess is as good as mine. All she does is bring up the past they share. I don't give a damn about none of it."

"Did you talk to him about it?"

"Yeah."

"And what does he say?"

"Told me to block her."

"And?"

"The bitch must be Verizon cause she got a bunch of different numbers. I'm tired of hearing from her. If she wants him, she can go and have him, why does she have to bother me?"

"Wanna meet up with her and fuck her up?" I laughed because Free was serious as hell. "I'm serious."

"No. We're mamas and don't need to be sitting in jail because we beat her ass."

"Shit, bail money is nothing."

"It's not, but I'm not going to give in to what she wants. She wants to meet with me, and I refuse to give her that. Priest slept with her, not me. I don't need to speak or address anything with the bitch."

"You should tell him that he needs to make her stop. It seems like it starts and ends with him, so he needs to put her in his place," I tossed my phone to the other side of the couch.

"Yeah, we'll talk about it when he comes over later."

"Later, eh?"

"He comes to put Yasmine to sleep. I be in my bed watching TV, and he says good night and I lock the door behind him."

Nothing was happening with me and Priest and I wished Free stopped wishing and praying for it to happen. She understood that he fucked up, yet secretly she was still wishing and hoping that we would fix things and make it work. Everyone wanted that and I understood that, still, I couldn't get over what he did to me and I didn't think I could get over it. I would always be wondering if he was cheating on me, or if an old friend pops up, I would wonder if there was something more. Lavern harassed me like I was the problem. She met me, knew I was with him and still chose to sleep with him knowing he belonged to another woman. Just because they had history didn't mean that she could do what she did. Nonetheless, I was the one being harassed like I ripped her happy family apart.

Freedom and Samoor stayed over for a few more hours before she headed home. When Somali called and told her that their nanny wasn't feeling too good, she darted out the door to get home to her babies. I loved how she accepted Rain like her own. She came back to Staten Island with two kids, and now she had four. Shit, if she got some dick in Belize, she might have five when she left the country. I locked the door behind them and went to shower while Yasmine was swinging gently in her swing. She was awake with the pacifier sticking out of her mouth. I loved that my baby didn't need to always be asleep for me to get things done. She could be in her bouncer, swing or bed looking at the ceiling and wouldn't cry. The only time she cried is when she wanted some milk.

I held the door opened for Priest around nine. Yasmine was already sleep and I had told him via text message, yet he still insisted on coming over to kiss her goodnight. I closed the door behind him as he kicked his shoes off and headed to her nursery. I leaned in the doorway as I watched him gently pick her up and sit in the rocking chair. He kissed her forehead a few times, then cradled her while rocking in the chair.

"Daddy had a hard day today, but seeing you has made it all worth it," he spoke softly to her. "I missed you, Yasmine," he cooed.

Priest was an amazing father. Hell, I knew he would be. He was always here to kiss her goodnight and never missed a night. It didn't matter what he had going on, he made a way to see or speak to his daughter. He would call just to hear her light baby snores and it annoyed the hell out of me. Then, I thought about if I had a baby father who didn't give a damn. He wasn't one of those fathers and I couldn't be mad because he wanted to always spend time with his baby. If things didn't go down the way they did, I knew we would have been happy. I often thought about how things were so perfect once upon a time ago. Everything seemed like stuff was going down the right path for us. Marriage probably would have been next after Yasmine. Now, we were living in two different homes and just trying to do the best for our daughter. It was funny how shit happened.

"You good?" I noticed he was now looking and talking to me. Priest always asked if I was fine, even if I ignored him, it was nice that he asked me.

"Just tired. I had a long day," I yawned and folded my arms.

"I miss you," he revealed.

"I bet you do," I turned and walked into my bedroom. Tonight wasn't the night for him to tell me how much he missed me.

Was it crazy that I missed him too? I missed feeling him inside of me and screaming his name. You didn't know what you had until you couldn't get dick whenever you wanted. Did I miss him emotionally? Probably, but I would never admit that to him. You didn't get to stomp on my heart and think that a few *sorrys and miss yous* would solve everything.

"Justice, I love the fuck out of you and I'm sorry that I even did that dumb shit. I'm not blaming no one because it was me that made the decision to fuck around. I made a stupid judgement call and tried to use our small fight as a reason to justify my cheating. You've always been real with me, even when I didn't want to hear it, I should have been the same with you. You didn't deserve what I did to you."

I stood there and looked at him. He was saying all the right things, but that wouldn't be enough this time. Saying all the right things wouldn't allow my heart to open and allow him back inside. The crazy thing was that I believed everything he was saying. I could tell he would never hurt me again and he had learned his lesson, still, a part of me wouldn't allow me to let him in.

"Go home, Priest," I pushed his chest out of my bedroom. If he took another step further, I don't know what would have happened.

"Have a good night, Justice. I love y'all," he said and headed toward the door. As I took the door knob in my hand to let him out, he turned around and kissed me on the lips. "I want this more than I want to breathe. I fucked up and I'm not expecting you to forget, but I need your forgiveness," he said.

"Goodnight," was all I could muster out. Tomorrow Yasmine had an appointment and I had to get up to make sure the Uber arrived in time.

MORNINGS WITH A CHILD was never easy. I remember when I was able to shower, sit for ten minutes in my robe and even have time for a cup of tea. Now, I was barely able to run a brush through my hair because my child commanded all my attention. She looked adorable, meanwhile I walked into places looking like I had been beat by roadkill. This morning wasn't no different. Yasmine had her appointment and I had scheduled my Uber last night before I went to bed. Each time I looked at my app, I didn't see the black Uber X I had booked near my house. I hated waiting on people, and this was a prime example of why I tried to do everything myself.

Priest had a meeting with Kiki's therapist this morning, so he had to miss Yasmine's appointment. Her doctor's office was hard to get into, so I had to take what they gave me. He made me promise that I would keep him on the phone while the doctor spoke so he wouldn't miss anything. It was comical how he thought I couldn't get Yasmine to her appointment and fill him in on it without having him on the phone.

Come downstairs. He sent me a message and I sighed. He probably got out of the appointment early and decided to come get me. Since the Uber wasn't here, I had no other choice but to get inside his car.

I gathered up all of Yasmine's things and my purse before heading downstairs. When I got downstairs, I didn't see him. Instead, I saw a Rolls Royce truck with a bow sitting in the assigned parking spots. A man was standing beside it, and that's when I noticed the truck with the trailer parked on the opposite of the street. I dialed Priest so quick my nail almost came off.

"You see it?" he answered.

"What is this?"

"You shouldn't have to borrow everyone's car. I'm sorry it's late, but I had to pull some strings to get this shipped from Calabasas."

"A... R...rolls Royce truck? This is too much," I stammered.

"Justice, you deserve this truck and more. I'm sorry for putting you through all of this. Having Yasmine should have been the happiest day of your life and I fucked that up. This can never make up for that, but I promise I'm not going to stop until I make it up to you, ma."

"Ma'am, can you sign for this? I have the keys right here and then it's all yours. Mr. Mooney paid extra for it to come this early," the short Italian man next to the truck told me.

"Y... you don't even have this car. I can't take this car," my hands shook as I signed my name and dated on the dotted line.

"You're the only person in Staten Island with this shit. I made sure when I got it delivered to the Rolls Royce dealership in Jersey. He has a few clients in Staten Island still on the waitlist."

"Priest, what did you do?" I giggled and accepted the keys from the man. "I don't even know how to drive this thing," I was floored that he pulled something like this. Last night, he didn't tell me that he was doing this.

"I want my ladies to ride in style, is that so wrong? Despite what is going on with you and me, I always want to make sure you're safe with my daughter. You like to be independent and I get that, but I don't want you and my daughter riding around in an Uber.

"Thank you, Priest. It is too much, but I appreciate you getting us a car."

"I love you, Justice. It's nothing. Let me get back to this appointment. Can we do lunch after Yas' appointment?"

"I'll think about it," I smirked and ended the call.

"He loves you. The way he yelled for me to get over here this morning, that man loves you," the man told me.

After the man showed me how to work the truck, me and Yasmine were on our way. The stares we got when we pulled up to the light, or when I chose to valet park the truck at her appointment was crazy. People had a million questions that I didn't have answers to. I didn't know half of what this truck did. All I knew was that I saw it on Instagram and was intrigued by it. I had never told Priest that I wanted this truck either. As over the top as the truck was, I was happy that I didn't have to wait around for an Uber or borrow someone's car to get around. As much as I liked the truck, I knew that I couldn't use this as an everyday truck. I checked in and waited for the nurse to call us to the back. My phone rang and I was hesitant about even answering.

"Hello?"

"Justice McGurry?"

"Yes, who is speaking?"

"My name is Patty Morgan, I'm Mr. Mooney's real estate agent. Are you available to pick up the keys to your condo today?"

"Excuse me?" I was so confused when she mentioned condo.

"Yes, Mr. Mooney purchased you a three-bedroom condo in a gated community. He said it was a push present for the baby.

Congratulations, by the way. It's ready to be moved in, you just need to pick up the keys from me today."

"Uh, can I call you back?" This had to be a dream. Priest couldn't have bought me a new damn condo and a car in the same day. I had to be dreaming.

11

Priest

"I know you hate going to therapy, but do you think it's helping you?" I questioned Kiki, as we drove home.

She shrugged her shoulders and continued to look out the window as we drove. I wanted the Kiki that laughed, was silly and was so passionate about dance. It seemed like overnight she changed, and I didn't know how to get her back. When I got the call about her trying to kill herself in school, I wanted to fall to the ground and beg God to give me the answers and guidance to watch over her. I had been so occupied with my personal life that I had missed the signs. She never wanted to go to school, stayed to herself and dropped out of dance a few months ago. I thought she just outgrew it like Love did, so I didn't stress it. Thinking back, those were all signs of a child going through something and not wanting to talk about it. Her sisters even missed it and I felt like shit because I was supposed to be there to protect her.

"Come on, this doesn't work unless you talk to me," I nudged her and tried to get a smile out of her.

"Ro, I don't know. I go because you think it's what is best. I'm not going to try and kill myself again, and I'm tired of having to talk about it," she sighed and leaned her head on the window.

"I'm sorry," I apologized.

"For what?" she looked at me confused.

"I haven't been the best uncle and provider. I allowed shit in my personal life to take over and I ignored your cries for help."

She started sniffling and that's when I noticed she was crying. "I don't fit in nowhere. When I'm around the white kids, I'm the black girl with big hair and dark skin. Then, when I'm with the black kids, I'm the black girl who talks white and think she's better than everyone. I didn't ask to have Gucci bookbags, get dropped off in fancy cars and talk like this. It's hard trying to fit in, especially when boys..." she allowed her voice to trail off.

"When what, Kiki?"

"I don't want to talk about it, Ro," she pleaded with me.

"Tell me."

She sighed and looked out the window. "Me and a boy were going out and went to the bathroom during class, and we messed around. His friends were in the stalls and took pictures of me."

"What the fuck?" I blurted. When she allowed her voice to trail off, I didn't think that was what she was going to say. "Kiki, why didn't you tell me?"

"For what? I told my teachers and the principal about them posting me on social media, and no one did anything. I don't ever want to go back to the school, Ro. Put me in public school, I don't care," she sobbed.

I made a sharp left and headed to her school. "I'm pissed you didn't tell me this shit sooner. Or maybe I'm pissed that I didn't notice the signs sooner. Either way, I'm pissed," I spoke through gritted teeth.

As much as my nieces got on my nerves and were dramatic

as fuck, they were my princesses and didn't deserve to be hurt the way Kiki had been. Especially since she was a good ass kid. The girl never bothered anybody and was a good student. I paid out the ass for this school and they were due to receive her tuition check next month for the next school year. Not once did they tell me she came to them with her concerns, or did they say anything when Kiss' ass was fucking in the bleachers in school. They placed all the damn blame on Justice, then fired her, but not once took accountability for the shit. It took me twenty minutes to make it to her school. When I did, I damn near jumped out of the car before I put it into park.

"Ro, do I need to go inside?"

"Yeah, let's go," I sternly told her and walked to the school building. As usual, I went through security and got a badge. It was lunch, so kids were filing in and out of the cafeteria. Kiki put her hood over her head, but that didn't stop someone from spotting her.

"Kiki, do you wanna live? Kiki do you love me?" they mocked her using Drake's lyrics. That shit had me so pissed I had to remember I could get jail time for fucking these group of boys up.

"Leave her alone. She's dramatic, who tries to kill themselves at school. Here's a hint, do it at home, loser." A girl came into the middle of the group with a smirk on her face.

"Let's just go, Ro," Kiki whispered, which pissed me off. These pale face bastards had the nerve to make light of something that was so important and serious.

I turned around and walked right over to them. "You love your mom?"

"Fuck you want to know for?"

I pulled my shirt up and showed my gun. "Say another thing to that one right there and I'll fucking put a hole in all of your moms' heads."

"My mom died already," the smart-ass little bitch had the

nerve to say. I guess she didn't get the glimpse at my gun, so I flashed it again. "I'll kill you instead."

"S...sorr...sorry," the main bitch ass stuttered.

"Don't let her brains and voice fool you, she got a whole bunch of niggas that will go to war for her and trust you don't want me to call them. One call, and you'll be wearing black," I hawked up spit and spit right in his face. I believed that spitting in someone's face was the worst thing you could do, but the fact that these were the kids responsible for me almost losing my niece, made me want to do it.

When I turned around, there was a teacher staring, but didn't say a word. Instead, she motioned for me to follow behind her. She opened the classroom door and then closed it behind me and Kiki.

"I've watched those kids pick on her every day at lunch. Their parents have donated a lot of money to this school, so they get away with murder."

"Not anymore. I want them held accountable for what the fuck they did to her," I was still on one, so she was probably scared because I was yelling.

"Honey, I'm sorry you thought suicide was the only way out. If you ever need to talk, my office is down the hall."

"She doesn't even need to worry about that, she ain't coming back to this school," I said and left her classroom. She pulled me in here to tell me how those kids were basically God cause their parents donated. I guess they didn't know who the fuck I was.

Since my niece felt her life didn't matter and they felt the same way, I would shoot up their homes so they could get the point of fear and sorrow that Kiki must have felt while going through this. The principal's assistant was outside at her desk and smiled when she saw me walk up. That same smile faded when she saw me walk right into the office where the principal was having his lunch.

"Excuse me, I'm on lunch."

"Excuse me, I'm ten minutes from fucking you up," I mocked and stared at him with menacing eyes.

"Woah, woah, what is going on here? Katherine?" he called his assistant, who slowly walked inside the office. I could tell Katherine didn't want none of the smoke this pink looking muthafucka was about to receive.

"He just came in, Sir," she explained and then closed the door behind us.

"Can this be scheduled at a later date? I'm having lunch right now," he sat back down and cut into his steak.

I took my hand and brushed the whole meal onto the floor, sending his papers, phone and computer mouse with it. "Katherine, please call security."

"Katherine, call security and I'll fuck you up my damn self," I pressed the same button he had pressed seconds before. "My niece attempted suicide on this campus and you're enjoying a fucking steak lunch."

"Kiki Mooney?" he asked, like he didn't already know.

"She came to you weeks before and told you about the fucking inbred ass munchers by the lunchroom. There was video showing her body and neither of you done nothing about it."

"She willingly participated in relationship with one of the students."

"Doesn't mean she wanted to be fucking recorded!" I barked at him and he damn near jumped back into the window behind him.

"We spoke to the students and they said there was no video. What else did you want me to do? It seemed like a petty adolescent fight."

"Did Kiki hanging herself in the fucking boy's bathroom sound like a petty adolescent fight? I pay out the ass to make sure my kid not only receives good education but is protected and you failed her."

"We followed all the protocol."

"So, in that protocol, was there something that said to call the parent? You all failed to let me know what was going on."

"Yes, we failed to bring this to your attention. We figured she would fill you in at home."

I paced the floor. "I'm ten minutes from breaking your fucking jaw."

"Sir, I understand you're upset, but violence isn't the answer."

"But, posting child porn on the internet is?" I sat in the chair in front of him. My hand was itching to pull the gun out and pop one right in his head. With Kiki standing here, I didn't want to put her through any more traumatic shit.

"If she chooses to return next year, we'll do a better job."

"Nah. She not coming back, and neither are those little assholes."

"Excuse me?"

"You're going to expel them, and..." I grabbed his phone and opened it. "If you so happen to accept them back next year, I'll put a bullet in her head. It takes nothing to make it up to Yale," I showed him the picture of his screensaver of a girl in a Yale sweatshirt.

He gulped hard. "It's not easy. Their family has been donating to this school for years," he stammered.

"Okay," I walked to the door and opened it. "Pick out a pink casket, she looks like the type to like some dramatic shit like that. Want me to tell her anything before I do it? Nah, nah, I'll just do it quick and easy," I laughed and headed out the door.

We were almost down the hall when I heard my name being called. "Mr. Mooney! I...I'll do...I'll draw up the papers today!" he hollered down the hallway.

"I'll be back to check this week," I winked.

Me and Kiki got into the car and I took her to grab something to eat before we headed home. "Why did you do all of that?" she wondered out loud.

"For you and your sisters, I'll air this entire world out. You mean the world to me and when someone hurts you, they hurt me... I don't know about you, but I don't like being hurt."

"Thank you, Ro," she leaned her head on my shoulder as I drove us home. Kiki had been my baby girl for a long time, so whenever someone fucked with her, I had to step in and make sure that she was good. When I think about how I could have been burying her, my mind went dark and I wanted to kill everyone who was involved. She was my angel and I would always protect her.

"Always and forever."

We need to talk. Justice sent me a text message and I sighed. Whenever she initiated a talk, I knew the shit wouldn't be good.

"You feel like going to see Yasmine?"

"Yeah, we can," she said, not taking her head up from my shoulder.

I headed to Justice's crib and smiled when I saw her new whip parked out front. There were a few people snapping pictures in front of it. Justice deserved everything that I was planning on giving her. When I sat back and thought about how I did her, I was fucking disgusted with myself. How could I allow myself to slip back into something with Lavern, especially when I had a woman like Justice waiting for me? Show me a perfect man and I'll show you a liar. I'm not perfect and I never pretended to be. I make mistakes and I happened to make one that messed up my life and a chance with the love of my life. Justice didn't deserve the shit I did to her and I beat myself up every day because of that shit. Even if we never got back together, I would always make sure she was good and that I supported her and Yasmine in whatever they both wanted to do. She did so much to bring our baby into this world and how did I repay her? By showing up with lipstick on me from another woman.

I knocked on the door and it took a minute for her to answer. When she did, she had a maxi dress that dusted the floor, and her hair was pulled up in a ponytail. "Hey Kiki!" she hugged Kiki tightly.

"Hey Jus, I missed you."

"I missed you so much. How are you?"

"Better," Kiki smiled.

"Let me tell you something, the next time you try and leave us, me and you are going to have a problem. I should have been there for you and I'm sorry that I wasn't," she apologized and hugged her again.

"Thank you," Kiki said. "Is Yasmine sleep?"

"Girl, no. She in that crib making noise because it's food time. Take the bottle on that table and you can feed her. Be careful."

"Okay," she said and went to the back to feed Yasmine.

"Damn, you look good," I licked my lips and looked at her up and down. "Ass poking out, shit, Yasmine just added to your beautiful curves."

"I need to lose some weight, she gave me too much booty and breast," she laughed. This was good. She shared a laugh with me. "Anyway, what are these keys?" she held up the keys to her condo.

The condo was near the house in a community called the Yacht Club; it was a ten-minute walk from my house. As much as she wanted to be independent, I couldn't sleep knowing she wasn't protected. Since she didn't want to sleep under my roof, it brought me comfort to know that she was sleeping in a gated community with my daughter every night. I put everything in her name, so even if we didn't get back together, the place was hers and I paid for it in cash.

"I got you a new place. I know you wanted to be independent, but you have to be smart."

"I am smart. My neighborhood is safe and you're the one who got that elaborate ass car. I was good with a damn Nissan," she huffed.

"This place is safe and is in a gated community. You mentioned putting roots down for Yasmine, and this is the place you can do it at."

"Priest, I don't want to live in a house that you own. Even if I don't own this place, the rental agreement is in my name."

"I put everything in your name. Did you even look at the folder she handed you?"

She grew quiet. "Why would you do that?"

"Because I support you wanting to be independent and wanting to do it on your own. I just want to make sure that while you're being independent, you're being safe too," I walked closer to her. "I know when we got together everything moved so fast, so we didn't get that chance to actually feel what it felt like to be together, but not live together. This condo is yours forever. If we don't work out, I don't want you to feel like you have to move, it's yours. Because, the next time you move out, you'll be moving into a bigger crib and you'll be my wife."

"You sound so sure of yourself."

"I know what I did, and I know what I have to do to get back what I lost."

She walked over to the couch and sat down, crossing her legs. "About what you did... the calls and messages are getting out of hand," she spoke about Lavern.

Lavern must have got her number out of my phone when I was asleep. Even if, I didn't see what her reason was for contacting Justice. She had nothing to do with what we had going on. If Lavern was mad with anyone, she should have been angry with me, not Justice.

"I'm gonna meet up with her and tell her to stop contacting you. This shit is crazy that she's even reaching out to you."

"No, I want to meet with her. There's obviously a reason she keeps calling me, and not you."

I understood that Justice wanted to put an end to all of this, but meeting with Lavern wasn't a good idea. If her ass kept calling and contacting her, then that meant that she was tripping and I didn't want anything to happen to Justice because of it. I wouldn't be able to forgive myself if something happened to her because of some shit that I dragged her into.

"Nah, I don't think that's a good idea."

"I don't care what you think. This woman has harassed me for weeks and you don't think I have nothing to say to her?"

"I'm not saying that. I just can't risk something happening to you."

"She's not dangerous. Your dick is good, but not good enough to go to prison over," she side eyed me.

"Word? That's how you feeling?" I laughed.

She chuckled, then messed with the ends of her ponytail. "In all seriousness, she needs to stop contacting me and if that means I need to go and sit down with her to see why, then it's something that I'm willing to do."

"Then, I'm going to come with you."

"Nope."

"Justice?"

"Priest?" she countered.

"You need someone to come with you."

She rolled her eyes. "I'm a grown ass woman. Watch your daughter. That's all I need you to do right now."

I sighed and leaned back on the couch. "When you gonna move into your new place?"

"How do you know I'm gonna like it? I haven't even seen the place yet."

I looked around her apartment. "No offense, that shit nicer than this."

She hit me on the shoulder. "Excuse you? My apartment is cozy and it's mine."

"That condo is yours too and hella cozy."

"I'll go this week and see if I like it or not."

It felt nice seeing her being able to crack a smile. Since everything happened, she wore this stone face and if it wasn't the stone face, she had this look like she was about to cry if one thing went wrong. The fact that she let me sit back on her couch and hold a conversation longer than five minutes told me that we were making baby steps.

"Ight. Let me know how you like it."

"Uh huh. I have a question," she asked and turned to look me in the eyes. I sat up and gave her my undivided attention.

"What's up?"

"Was I not enough? What was I lacking that you found in Lavern?"

I dropped my head because I never wanted her to feel like it was her fault. At first, I blamed our argument and the foul shit she said, but I knew that wasn't the reason for me doing what I did. It was nothing that Justice did that made me do the shit that I did to her.

"Ma, you were more than enough. Shit probably more than I was used to. You bring so much to the table and maybe a piece of me got scared. Then, Lavern popped back up and I found comfort in having someone that knew me back them. I don't know, I'm rambling," I took a breath. "Truth is, Lavern was a small piece of my sister. Yes, the girls are too, but when I saw her, I thought back to all the times we would kick it in our old apartment with Sandy. A nigga would give up anything to be that teenager who had the world at his fingertips. It's not an excuse, but it's the reason that I gravitated toward Lavern. I also learned, that as much as I would give up being that teenager again, I'm not him anymore. I have grown and experienced shit and Lavern is just that... the past."

"I hear all that you're saying, but how can I believe you? How can I believe that she won't be a problem down the line? You did something so heart-breaking to me and I'm trying hard to forgive and not let the hate take over my heart."

I reached out and grabbed her hand. "My word doesn't mean much right now. I put it on our daughter's life that if you give us a fighting chance, I'll never do no shit like that again. Me and Lavern are done, and I put that on my own life. I just want to make you happy and raise our daughter together."

"It's some things I have to think about. In the meantime, just be there for your daughter. She needs you more than anything else."

"You already know I'm gonna be there for her. I want to be there for the both of you," I kissed her hand.

She smiled and looked away. "Just fix it," was all she said before she got up from the couch and went into Yasmine's nursery.

I nodded my head. If she said that I needed to fix it, then I was going to fix it. Justice and Yasmine meant everything to me, and I had finally got what I wanted. Us, niggas were stupid. We could get the best woman in the world and our stupid asses would fuck up because we were scared. Men were macho and felt like we could take over the world. When it came to women, especially one that had her shit together, we were scared shit-less. A woman that had her shit together and didn't need you, was a woman that we wanted, yet feared. Why? Because she didn't have to put up with our bullshit. She had options and as quick as her stilettos walked into our lives, she'd walk right back out. Justice had a degree, her own business and had her future ahead of her. She didn't need me and made that clear when she moved out of my house and never looked back. It took one thing for me to do for her to toss her bags over her shoulder and build a life without me. If my woman told me to fix it, then I was going to fix it and make it work.

We need to talk, I sent Lavern a text message.

You know my address.

Bet.

I LET two days slip by before I found the courage to bring myself back to Lavern's apartment. The other day was nice and peaceful. It was exactly what me and Kiki both needed. Justice cooked dinner, we watched movies and I got to put my daughter to sleep without having to knock on the door and being let in. On the ride home, I could tell that Kiki missed Justice. Her own mood changed, and she seemed to be in better spirits since we spent the day with her. Justice didn't know the hold she had over me and the girls. She was that sparkle that we needed in our lives since Sandy left. Everything in my spirit told me that I shouldn't have come to Lavern's apartment. I had this feeling and I tried to shake it off since I woke up this morning on Justice's couch. I came over to put Yasmine to sleep and I ended up falling asleep with her on my chest while sitting on the couch.

When I woke up this morning, she put a blanket over me. I peeked into her room and saw she and Yasmine were still asleep, so I took her spare key and dipped out to head home to shower and get ready to meet with Lavern. She had to know that what we had was years ago and that we couldn't continue that shit. We both had changed and had things going on in our lives. She was getting divorced and I wanted to eventually marry Justice. Not to mention, we both had kids that we had to take into consideration. As much as I made her remember the old days, we had to be smart and realize that our young years wasn't who we were now. We were two different people and outside of sex, we had nothing in common anymore.

I knocked on her door and stood back. She turned the locks and the door opened. "Hey," she greeted and held the door opened.

I walked in and looked around. "Your daughter here?"

"No, she's with her father," I found it weird that her ass never had her daughter. She was here that one time and I had never saw her again. "You can take a seat in the living room. Want some water?"

"Yeah. I'll take some," I replied and sat down on the couch. She returned with two bottles of water and sat on the opposite couch.

"What did you want to talk about?"

"Why do you keep hitting up Justice?"

She shrugged her shoulders. "Because I can," I thought she would deny the shit. It was the complete opposite. Her ass was sitting here looking like she was proud of doing the shit.

"How old are we? You playing on her phone as a grown woman is corny, Lavern."

She took a few gulps of her water and stared at me briefly before she spoke. "Corny? What's corny is how she ends things with you and you get scared and stop messing with me. How can you break off what we had?"

"What we fucking had was years ago, Lavern!" I hollered. "I was a fool to even think that I could get back what we used to have."

"No, you weren't. We could. Ro, we were so good together."

"*Were.*"

"You are choosing her because she has your child. If you loved her, you wouldn't have come running to me every chance you got."

I laughed. "Vern, every time we linked was because you hit me up. You wanna repaint what happened, but you called me each time your husband pissed you off. Stop making it what it wasn't."

"I'll continue to play on her phone."

"When did you become this fucking petty?"

"The moment I was in a fucking psyche ward because of the shit you did to me. You broke up with me and that shit broke my heart. I couldn't eat, sleep or do anything. My life felt like it had no purpose. Then, you have the nerve to have this bitch and make her happy."

"Nah, you tripping. This happened years ago, Lavern. How the fuck are you blaming her for what happened between us more than ten years ago?"

"Because we could have been happy together."

"So, you lied about college and shit... you been in a fucking looney bin?"

"No. I got better. I was going through severe depression. After a year, I got my shit together and took college classes at a community college. That's where I met my husband. Life was good, but I always thought about you and the girls."

"What we had was magical, when we were younger. We loved hard and yeah it was too intense for how young we were. Still, years passed, and I thought about you from time to time, but I did what I did so you could go on and be great. If I didn't, you would have stuck around to help me. I wanted you to go to college and accomplish your dreams," I had never told her why I ended things with her.

She stopped messing with her water bottle and looked at me. "Are you serious?"

"Yes. You loved me and the girls that much and I knew you would give up going away to college to help me with the girls. I did it to look out for you, Lavern, not to hurt you. I'm sorry that I hurt you because I didn't know any other way to get you to leave."

She wiped away tears. "I've never felt heartbreak like the one you gave me. Not even with my husband. You're the love of my life and I mean that. Moving back to Staten island, I planned to look for you, so when we ran into each other at my job, I knew that meant we were supposed to make it work."

"If I didn't have Justice, then maybe that's what the universe would have been telling us to do. I have love for you and want you to know sending you away that night in the hallway was the hardest thing I have ever had to do. I couldn't be selfish. What we shared was the past and we need to focus on being better for the future. I hurt a woman that means a lot to me because I was chasing a high from my past. I don't know if you and your husband can work things out, but fix it, if it can be fixed."

She continued to wipe her tears away. "I'm sorry. I'm sorry for all of it."

"All that matters is how we move on from this. I want you to be happy and I want you to give your daughter a good life. Keep going to college because it's never too late, Vern," I stood up.

She stood up and I hugged her tightly. "I love you, Ro."

"I love you too, Vern. You gotta move on and stop putting your blame and hurt onto Justice. We hurt her, not the other way around."

"You're right," she agreed.

She walked me to the door, and we hugged once more before I left her apartment. I prayed this talk would help her get over what we had. If it didn't, then maybe Justice would have to sit and talk to her. I prayed that it wouldn't come to that.

12

Freedom

Belize

WE HAD BEEN in Belize for two weeks and everything felt so peaceful. Gyson had flew his doctor here to give him his treatments and teach a local doctor to administer them. Everything felt so perfect and I was glad that we decided to come and bring the kids. Things had been so stressful at home and seeing how much fun they were having made it all worth it. Although we had been gone for two weeks, I still brought work with me and would sneak away while the kids played and Gyson napped to get some work done. If I could live here, I would. The food, the sun and the peace made me not want to return back to the states ever again. Gyson still got weak after his treatments, but he was pushing through. We didn't do much except sit outside and watch the kids swim. On date nights, we would go out to a local restaurant and enjoy each other to the fullest. Ms. Winnie was enjoying her time and held down the kids when we were having alone time. Everything about Belize made me wake up with a huge smile on my face each morning. The one thing that I wanted was some dick.

I had brought the pills secretly. Gyson wanted to have sex more than anything and nothing helped. I was tired of bouncing on a soft dick. We had tried everything that google suggested, except sticking something up his ass. He refused and damn near tried to attack me when I tried to do it when he was asleep. Listen, I was desperate and wanted some dick. It had been so long that I didn't know how it felt anymore. Still, he refused the pills, even after his doctor said that they were safe and natural to use. Truthfully, I think he was scared to have sex. Maybe he forgot how to work it or something. It was some reason why he didn't want to take the pills. It was hard being in paradise and not getting my back blown out. Ms. Winnie took Samoor into her suite every night so we could have alone time. It wasn't like Gyson didn't try and please me. He would eat my pussy until I creamed nearly every night. Yet, it wasn't the same to me. I wanted to feel him, connect and do all the nasty things that we used to do.

"Mommy, what are you making?" Rain asked, as I was making lemonade. I had the crushed pills hidden to the side of the bowl of lemonade.

"Lemonade, you want some?" I asked her.

"Yes please," she flashed a bright smile at me. I loved this little girl so much. She had the brightest smile and was the politest kid I had ever met.

I poured her some lemonade. "Where's your sister?"

"In the pool with Samaj, they are battling on who is faster."

"And who is winning?"

"Samaj."

"And who is whining?"

"Somali," she giggled.

"And where is your baby brother?"

"Ms. Winnie is feeding him. Mommy, can you have me another baby sister?"

I kneeled down and kissed her cheek. "We have so much going on right now and Samoor is still a baby. Maybe in a year we can try and have a baby sister just for you... okay?"

"Okay. I'll ask daddy just in case to see what he says," she skipped away.

"Wait, where is your daddy?"

"Sleeping outside by the pool," she yelled as she continued to skip out of the kitchen. Everyone was cooling by the pool and I was in here about to drug my damn man.

I sprinkled the pill into the lemonade and sat it to the side while I put the salmon in the oven, and then made vegetable casserole to go with it, and for Gyson, since he was now vegan. When I was done, I set the oven on low and went outside and gave the kids their tray of lemonade. Ms. Winnie took hers and continued to feed Samoor. Gyson was over in the shade napping, so I brought his cup over to him.

"Hey baby, here's something to drink. Don't want you getting dehydrated out here," I gently woke him and sat in the fold out chair beside him.

"Thank you," he stirred from his sleep. His eyes landed on my bathing suit. It was an orange bathing suit with huge cut outs on the side. After Samoor and finding out that Gyson had cancer, the stress ate away at that baby fat. You couldn't tell me that I wasn't feeling myself. "Damn, you look good," he complimented.

"Thank you, boo," I smiled and put my sunglasses on and laid there to soak up this sun.

The kids splashed in the water, and Rain yelled about the twins not allowing her to win in the volley ball game they started. Samoor was cooing with Ms. Winnie. Everything felt so good and I wanted to capture this moment forever. Eventually, we would have to go back home and deal with the doctor's appointment that would determine if Gyson was in remission or would need more treatments. It was one that I was nervous about. I wanted so bad for him to beat this cancer and get back to being himself. I wanted that for him more than anything else in the world. These past few months had been hard on him mentally and physically. There was nothing I could do except be there for him. He told me that was all he needed, yet I felt like I should or could do more. Each time I tried to do more he told me that was all he needed from me. Just me being there for him made his day. Gyson was the king of our castle and it wouldn't be the same if we lost him. Cancer didn't care if you were the most paid, handsome or the fact that you were a kingpin. When it hit, it hit and often time you were too tired to fight the battle that it put up. I was proud to say that Gyson fought that shit like a nigga in the street. Even on his weakest days, he was still fighting with all the strength he had left.

"Ms. Winnie?" I called over to her.

"Yes, baby?"

"I put the food in the oven. If I fall asleep, can you keep an eye on it," I told her.

"Of course," she replied and sat Samoor in his little playpen. He laid flat on his back while kicking his legs because she had sat him down. That little boy was so spoiled. Because he was the baby of all the kids, he was always in someone's hands. So, when you put him down, he would throw a fit because he wasn't used to it.

"Thanks," I replied and closed my eyes.

I don't know how long I had been asleep, but I felt Gyson tapping me. "Baby, wake up," he continued to shake me.

I leaned up and looked and saw the kids making smores with Ms. Winnie. The sun was setting, and everyone was giggling and laughing. "Did you eat dinner? Why didn't anyone wake me up?"

"Because you never get to sleep running behind all of us," I noticed the cashmere blanket draped across my legs.

"That sleep felt so good. Are you ok—"

"Daddy, can you give me another baby sister?" Rain came over with chocolate all over her mouth.

"Shit, daddy about to make you one right now," he said. "Go with Ms. Winnie," he told her. Rain skipped back over there and that's when I noticed the bulge in his pants.

"Ohhhh, it's working?" I acted like I had no parts in his hard dick.

He stood up, grabbed me up from the chair and carried me into the house while I giggled. He was so horny that we didn't even make it up to the bedroom. He closed the laundry room door and sat me on the dryer. My pussy craved and called out to him. He pulled his trunks down and slipped my bathing suit to the side and slipped right inside of me. I tossed my head back as he slammed into me like a jack hammer does concrete. The kids were occupied, and I could be as loud as I wanted to. When Gyson carried me inside, Ms. Winnie had a smile on her face, so she knew what was about to go down between the both of us.

I wrapped my legs around his body and grabbed around his neck. He leaned on the wall while I took control. This was what I wanted, and I had gone as far as to drug his ass to get it, so I was about to show him how much I missed feeling him on the inside of me. Gyson held onto my booty cheeks and allowed me to move my hips and pound my pussy onto his dick. I wanted to scream because it felt so good. He was out of breath and I could tell he was struggling to hold me up. I got down, grabbed his hand and we ran upstairs to our bedroom. I shut the door, pushed him on the bed and caressed his dick before I jumped on top of it. For a minute, I just sat there and took in how it felt sitting straight up into me. His dick was so big it felt like it was in my stomach. Having a dick so big lying beside you every night and not being able to have your way with it, did some things to do you.

"You went as far as to drug me to get this nut, show me what you working with," he chuckled.

"I don't know what you're talking about," I slowly started to ride his dick while holding onto his chest.

"I saw the pill residue on the side of the cup," he laughed, grabbed my waist tighter and flipped me on my stomach. He pulled my hair and shoved his dick into my dripping pussy. "You wanted this, didn't you?" I remained silent because I was doing somersaults in my damn head. "I don't hear you," he gripped my hair tighter.

"Yes, baby, I want it."

"How bad?"

"Bad as fuccccccck," I moaned when he pulled out and slapped that shit on my ass. He did it again and I screamed out because I needed this put inside of me. "Baddddddd, fuck me!!! Fuck me!!!!" I hollered.

With how loud I was, I was sure the kids heard me screaming like a damn lunatic. "Ight," he said and slammed himself inside of me. With one hand, he gripped my hair and with the other, he planted the palm of his hand firmly into the middle of my back. The pain and pleasure mixed had me tossing this ass back at him.

"Harder!" I screamed.

He let go of my hair and grabbed both sides of my waist and shoved his dick so far inside of me I was sure he had put one of his balls inside of me too. He pulled all the way out, and then slammed into me one good time and flipped me on my back. With one leg up, he held my leg up and continued to string the strings of my guitar below.

"Baby, this feels sooo gooood," I whispered because he had fucked my voice out of me. "Right there, right there," He had my leg up in the air, his thumb in my booty, and was stroking me with that big dick of his. When I started screaming again, he reached down and covered my mouth with his. Gyson Davis had every one of my holes closed and I felt like I was having an out of body experience. As much as I complained about being sexually frustrated, he was too, and I could tell. The way he stroked me slow and then sped up like he was punishing my pussy.

When I came, I shook, screamed and cried. Gyson leaned over me with his dick still inside of me as I had an orgasm. He pulled out and held me and kissed me while my body shook. Once it had passed, I looked into his eyes with so much happiness. I needed this more than he knew.

"Come finish me off," he demanded, and I went to the bottom of the bed and took his dick into my mouth. I pushed him to the back of my throat and hummed while sucking him like my favorite popsicle.

He held his hand on the back of my head and when it felt good, he would pull my hair and I knew to keep the same rhythm I had been going. "You like that?" I asked with my dick still in his mouth.

The vibration from my voice sent chills down his body. His toes were crawled up in a ball and he was holding onto the sheet with his free hand. "Shit, yeah, I like that shit," he moaned out and pushed my head further. I pulled his dick out of my mouth and spit on it a few times before I shoved it back down my throat. While I sucked on the tip, I jerked the shaft and flicked my tongue across his hole. I went back down and swallowed him whole while massaging his balls.

"I... I'm 'bout to nut," he stammered and pulled my head down. I felt his nut ooze out the head and I swallowed it down my throat. When I took his dick out of my mouth, I kissed the tip and then went to kiss him.

"How was that?"

"If the cancer doesn't kill me, you damn sure about to kill me," he laughed.

"Gyson Davis!" I hollered.

"I'm playing. Do me a favor."

"What?"

"Go in the top drawer and get me that box out," he directed. I got up with my bathing suit all twisted around my body. He damn near fucked the bathing suit off me.

I went to the dresser and grabbed the box. "What's this?" I asked, as I plopped beside him on the bed and handed him the box.

"Open it."

"What is this?" I cut my eyes at him. "I told you to stop buying me so much jewelry," I started to unravel the box.

"I think this is going to be the best piece I ever got you," he told me and I didn't know if I believed him or not.

"Uh huh. Every piece you have gotten was beautiful, so I don't know how you're going to top this," I smiled and opened the velvet black box. It was a ten-karat halo shaped diamond ring. The diamond was half a carat, still the ring was beautiful as hell. "What is this?" I asked, as I admired it in the box.

"Before you left and went to Atlanta, I had bought you an engagement ring. It was between a new transmission for my whip, or this ring, so I got the ring. I planned to do it on your birthday, but you left before that could happen. Your birthday is in two days, and I was going to wait until then, but I wanted you to have this ring now. It's small, and with the money I got I could buy you something way bigger with more carats, but it's something—"

"I don't want something bigger; I want this one," my voice cracked.

"I knew you would say that," he climbed off the bed; butt ass naked. I watched as he got on one knee, he grabbed the ring from me and held it up. "Freedom, we been through a lot of shit. You've always been the one for me. I'm tired of calling you my girl, I'm ready to call you my wife... will you marry me?" he asked, and I was a ball of emotions. I had been doing a good job of keeping it together, but once those tears fell down, I was crying like a big ass baby.

I was nodding my head yes before he could finish what he was saying. "Yes, yes, yes, I'll marry you!" I hollered.

Gyson slipped the ring onto my finger and I got down off the bed and grabbed his face with both hands. Kissing him, I pulled back and looked him in the eyes. "I love you so much."

"I love you too," I kissed him again while looking at the ring on my hand. I didn't care that it wasn't the biggest ring. I loved it because this ring held history to our relationship.

I jumped up and ran to the balcony where the kids were still messing with their smores. "Mommy is getting married!" I flashed my ring and they all jumped up and cheered.

I couldn't wait to be Ms. Davis.

13

Ghost

Belize

I⊤ ⊤ook me a whole week to pull everything together. Freedom was happy with just wearing my ring and wasn't sweating the wedding part. I guess she thought we would take that step whenever I was ready to help her plan. Little did she know, I had plans on marrying her right on the beach of our villa. When I told her that I wasn't letting her get away again, I meant that shit. I wasn't about to fuck up this time. Freedom was meant to be my wife and I was going to make sure that I did right by her and my kids. She had proved to me that she was here for me and nothing else. She didn't give a damn about the money or street cred I had. All she wanted was me; Gyson. While she had been spending time working and with the kids, I had been working on planning our wedding. I had everyone flying out today and they would land tonight. Free had no idea that I had been doing this.

She had been giving me that little pill so I had been fucking her brains out while Ms. Winnie handled stuff so she wouldn't grow suspicious of me. I tried to get Liberty, but she had a week left of her program, and then after she had outpatient every day, so it was no way she would be able to fly out. Even with her having to miss the wedding, she was so excited for Free and promised to keep quiet about it. I knew Free would be upset that she couldn't attend, so I had planned a special surprise for her. My mom was flying in with Justice, Staten, Priest and the girls. The only one that couldn't attend was Kiss, and that was because she and Reese had bought tickets to take Zamari to some paw patrol shit.

Last week, we had gone into town and I acted like I wanted to buy her this dress. She fell in love with it and I had the owner size her. I was able to use that to get my personal shopper to pick out a beautiful dress for her. It was too short time for something custom, but she promised that she would find me something that no one had. There were hairstylist and make-up artist due to come tomorrow morning to get her ready. I had to tell her today and I had been laying here trying to decide on how I would tell her. Her wedding dress was flying in with Justice, so I couldn't use that.

"Your daughters are so dramatic. Samaj acted like he tossed a bug on them and the way they performed and lock themselves in their rooms," she came into the room laughing with Samoor in her arms.

"Wonder where they get it from."

"You see... I'm gonna let that slide, but you better stop calling me dramatic," I reached for Samoor and she handed me over to him before taking a seat on the end of the bed. "Why are you still in bed?"

"I was comfortable. Staten called me and I had to handle a few things too, so I just laid here to do them."

"No work."

"I could say the same thing about you."

"Um, I haven't worked today... so quit it," she giggled.

"I gotta tell you something."

Her smile dropped and a serious expression appeared on her face. "What now, Gyson?"

"I'm gonna marry you tomorrow."

"Huh?"

"I've been planning our wedding behind your back. We're getting married tomorrow."

From her facial expression, I could tell she was trying to figure and sort everything I had just said to her out. "How? Our family isn't from here? We didn't get a marriage certificate."

None of that mattered when you had money. I had someone who was flying here on a favor to me just to officiate the wedding and make sure our marriage was legal. We would sign a paper here, and then once we got back to the united states, we had another paper to sign.

"What if I told you that I figured all of that out? Would you still marry me?"

"Without a doubt," she quickly replied.

"Ight. So, we're getting married tomorrow," I repeated myself.

"Gyson, you sound crazy. You've been sleeping and sexing me like crazy... how did you find time to plan a wedding?"

"I have my ways."

"Tell me those ways?" she folded her arms.

"Don't worry about it."

"Um, I need a dress, make-up and hair."

"Done, done, done."

"And the kids, what about them? Bet you didn't think about that, huh?" she was so sure that I forgot about the kids.

"Done," I smirked.

"Ugh, so what am I supposed to do? Show up?"

"Pretty much."

"Give me my damn baby," she rolled her eyes and them smiled. "Well, I'll go sit and wait for this to happen."

"Have fun."

"Gyson, tell me something!" she turned back around when she realized that I wasn't budging on the information I had. She would find everything out when it happened.

Justice, Priest and the girls were staying at his villa, and Staten and my mom were going to stay at his place. Free wasn't going to see them until tomorrow because they came in too late. I even had Messiah and Rasheed flying in. Messiah had been trying to link with me for a minute and I had been too consumed to reach back out. She understood I had a lot going on and told me she was going to come to the wedding. Despite whatever was going on with her and Staten, she would always show up for me, like I would for her.

"Go get me some lemonade and I'll make you tell me something," I winked.

"All you said is a word," she darted out the room. I knew she was going to toss Samoor in Ms. Winnie's arms, mix her little concoction up and be in here in under give minutes. I pulled my shorts off and waited for her freak ass to come back.

EVERYTHING ARRIVED PERFECTLY. Free was still asleep, so I went to check on Justice and Priest, since his place was closer to mine. While Free slept, I had staff putting out the flowers and decorating the area where we would be getting married. I knocked on the door and Justice opened the door holding Yasmine while breastfeeding her.

"We know Yasmine ate breakfast," I laughed.

Justice laughed. "She's greedy. You're getting married today, how do you feel?" she asked and all I could do was smile.

"Jus, I feel good. I couldn't sleep last night because I kept thinking about it. I'm ready to make her my wife."

She sat on the couch. "I'm so happy for the both of you. Free deserves all of this and more. You do too. Y'all have been through so much," she popped her breast back into her shirt and started burping Yasmine.

"I know, I know, I just want to make her happy for the rest of her life."

"Aw, look at this soft ass nigga," Priest chuckled as he came down the stairs. "You could have slept next to me; my bed was big enough."

"I was fine in the guest room," Justice replied. "You hungry?" she questioned and switched into the kitchen, leaving me and Priest alone.

"She still not giving you no play."

"At least she's not rolling her eyes at me," he shrugged. "I'm working double time and she making a nigga sweat while work for it."

"As she should. You fucked up, so you need to work hard and earn that place back in her heart."

"I hear you, but I need some pussy too."

"Isn't that the reason you're in this shit now?" I laughed.

"Fuck you!" he flipped his middle finger at me and laid across the couch. "How you feeling?"

"Good. I'm ready to go home and see what this doctor has to say about my labs and shit."

"Claiming good news always."

"Appreciate it, man."

"Always. Now, about you getting married. You ready for this? We can fuel up the jet and bounce," he kidded.

"I ain't never been so ready and sure of something in my life."

"You and Free has always been a good look. I can see the love and respect you both have for each other, and the way you both raise your children is admirable. If I'm half the father you are, I'll be good."

"You've been a father before I was even the father. Don't let the fact that they are your nieces fool you. You have been their father when Sandy died, and their own father didn't show up. Keep up the same thing with Yasmine and you got this. I'm telling you."

"Still, I feel like I failed them or some shit."

"As much as you want to shelter them from life, you can't. Kiki is going to be fine because you stepped in and got her the help she needed. Kiss took a different path, but she'll find her way back on the straight path. And Love, she's at the age where boys are life, you can't control that shit."

"I get so angry because I wanted Kiss to go to college. She had the grades to get into any Ivy League school she wanted to."

"That was your vision for her life, not hers. I want my boys to play pro ball and go to college, and I want my girls to go to college and start businesses... I also know when it's time for them to do that, the path I want for them might not be the path that they want to take, and I have to make peace with that."

"How do you make peace with that?"

"You think Sandy wanted this for you? She wanted you to finish college and you dropped out. That's how you make peace with it. You make peace by acknowledging that you were once in their shoes and never followed the path that was mapped out for you, so why should you force them to?"

"Wise man."

I shrugged. "I try."

"I want what you have so bad," he expressed. "The family life is something that I wanted bad as fuck, then I fucked it up."

"She's here, right? She could have stayed with us or with Staten, but she's here... She's giving you signals that you're not picking up. As much anger that she holds for you, she wants to fight for this too."

He nodded his head. "She's definitely making me work for it."

"She has to. And, when or if she decides to make it work with you, let her be. Let her live alone, let her continue being independent. Let her continue to build that life and don't toss marriage at her. Justice went from one relationship to the next and you were there to comfort her. Yet, she has never got the feeling of living on her own and getting comfortable with being alone."

"I hear you."

"You better. Don't bring up the idea of moving in together until you're ready to make her your wife. I don't mean what you just told me right now, I mean when you're ready to deal and accept that you have toxic traits and work on them. She has the same. Do the work and break those curses for the girls and Yasmine."

"I hear you."

"I know you do," I stood up and hugged him. "Let me get back to my villa before Free wakes up," I told them.

"Ight. Good looking for the talk."

"You already know... later, Justice."

"Later!" she yelled back.

PRIVATE BEACH, Belize,
6:30 PM

Why I Love You by Major played as Freedom came down the aisle that was littered with white rose petals. Her white pedicured foot kicked her long dress up so she could walk without tripping. Her mother held onto her arm as she tried to smile through the tears she was trying to hold back. Her hair was pulled up in a big French bun with a few pieces of hair hanging loose. The mermaid dress hung onto every curve she had, even the ones she may have been hiding. The dress showed all the perfection that I loved on her body. Justice had told me she had been emotional because Liberty couldn't come. My mama had called Free's mom and told her she needed to be here. She also told her if she didn't show up that she needed to act like she didn't have kids or grand-kids, because she would make sure to fill in her role forever. I didn't see when she saw her mother, but I heard from down the hall. She cried and screamed that her mother was able to attend and walk her down the aisle. Her mother held onto Free's arm and held the picture of her father in her other hand. The shit had me feeling emotional as fuck.

I don't know if her father would have approved of me being with her. I do know that I would always protect and love her while keeping him in the back of my mind. When he looked down, I wanted him to see that his daughter found someone with flaws yet loved the shit out of her. For the rest of her life, I wanted Free to know and feel what it felt to be loved by someone real. I wanted her to know that when she went to bed angry with me, I would still wrap my arm around her, no matter how many times she swatted me away. I wanted her to know that even when she wasn't feeling the most beautiful, she would always be the most beautiful woman to me. She had her flaws and I had mine too. Even with that, we still loved each other. *I love you so much.* She mouthed to me as she walked.

Staten stood to the side of me holding Samoor, and Samaj stood beside him. Somali and Rain stood on the other side with a chair that had Skype and Liberty was on the screen with a face full of make-up, as if she was attending the wedding in person. Free and her mother finally made it down the aisle and she handed me Free's hand and I helped her up the step.

"Who gives this woman away?"

"We do," her mother said and wiped away a tear. "Me and her father do," she looked at the sky with tears falling down her cheeks. "We do," she said again.

Justice stepped down and embraced her mother tightly. "It's

alright, mommy," she told her and walked her over to her seat and then stood beside the laptop with Liberty sobbing.

"She looks so beautiful. Like an angel," Liberty sobbed.

"You're going to make me cry, Lib," Justice sniffled. I could tell she was trying hard not to cry. Hell, it was hard for me not to cry.

"Ma, you look so fucking beautiful," I complimented and kissed her hand.

"Thank you, baby. Ho... how did you know about, Lib?"

I smirked. "She's your twin. You shared your mother's womb with her, it was vital that she was here, some way or another."

As the officiant spoke, all I could do was stare into my future wife's eyes. She held my gaze, as I thought about the future. All I wanted was to make my family happy. The streets used to make me happy, but fuck all that, I wanted to be the family man. In the streets, you only had two ways out; prison or death. I managed to cheat the game and I wanted to keep my word to making my family my priority. The simple life with my wife is what I wanted and desired. None of that street beef meant nothing to me. If I had to go through all of that to get to this moment, I would do it in a heartbeat.

"The couple wrote their own vows," the officiant announced.

"I'll go first," Freedom took the mic and looked at me. "I told myself I would cry and that I would write it down, but that would mean I would be writing forever. I love everything about you Gyson Davis. The way you love and protect your family is what makes me fall in love with you. How you can forgive and see the bright side of things is something I admire. I've watched you get out the bed every day and face the day, even though you don't want to. You teach our kids to never give up and to always show up and out. You love me like no man has ever. When I go to bed in your arms, I feel safe. If my daddy was alive, I know for a fact that you would have given him a run for his money," she chuckled. "I love you today, tomorrow and forever. My heart pumps for you and our children. I love you, baby," her hands were shaking as she wiped away her tears.

I grabbed her face and kissed her on the lips and then backed up, because it wasn't time for that. "Freedom Reign McGurry, the day you left my life I thought I would never see you again. I tried to find you in every woman I ran across and couldn't. When God put his stamp on you, he made sure that you were one in a million. There's not another woman that can match the fire that burns in your soul. I know, because I tried finding her. You run your business, raise our children and me, plus finds some time to do your weekend cleaning. Even with a nanny, you're never absent from our children's lives. Everyone that has met you, loves you. You've had plenty of times to run and never look back, but instead you ran toward me teaching me that the phrase, *'ain't nobody gonna have your back like your future wife does,'* is true" I sniffled. "When I found out about the cancer, I expected this to be too much and for you to run. I mean, you had a million things on your plate, so running away would have been the easiest thing for you to do. Instead, you pulled your pants up and has been there for me through it all. Not once have you complained, showed defeat or cried. Each obstacle that comes our way, you're right there ready to battle it before I can. Ma, I love you more than I love to breathe, and that's a lot. I promise, for the rest of my life that I will continue to make you happy and put your first. As your husband, I'll be ready to put a hole in anybody that causes you harm. I love you, Mrs. Davis."

Free was an emotional wreck. Tears and snot came down her face. Justice had to quickly get her together. "I lo... love.... Yo...you so much," she sobbed.

"For."

"Ever."

14

Listen to: Nobody Knows by The Tony Rich Project

The wedding, reception and all that shit was nice as fuck. I've seen weddings that were planned for a year never look like Free and Ghost's did. You could tell they were so happy. We partied on that beach until the next morning. All I thought about was Liberty. I wished she was here and with me. I missed her so much and knowing she would soon be marrying another nigga had me all in my feelings. When I flew back home, I stayed to myself for a bit because I needed to check my emotions at the door. Lately, Liberty had been on my mind and I just wanted to be with her. I wanted to make her happy like Ghost made Free. This new nigga couldn't make her happy like I could. Yeah, I admit, I wasn't perfect, and I had a lot of shit going with me. Still, I could promise to love and protect her.

It had been a month since I flew home from Belize. Free, Ghost and the kids had flown back last week for his appointment. His doctor had come to Belize to collect what she needed for his labs and his appointment next week would be when we found out if he was in remission. I ain't never been so nervous for something in my entire life. God knew I needed my brother here and these past few months had been the hardest for me to handle.

I haven't seen you. We really need to talk. Maliah had sent me another text message. I didn't know if it was depression or what that was going on with me. All I thought about was Liberty and ways on how I could make her mine again. I tried to pretend like I didn't care and that I wanted her to be happy, and that was only half true. I wanted her to be happy with me. This other nigga couldn't make her happy the way I could.

I'll come to your crib when I'm free. I felt bad for ignoring Maliah when she didn't deserve it. I hadn't even been by to see Satin because of my mood. I didn't feel like hearing anybody ask me what was wrong.

Oh wow. He's alive! she replied back. I tossed my phone onto the couch and leaned my head back.

Trac and Priest were making sure everything was running smoothly. I guess that was the perk of being the boss, you could do what you want and take as much time as you needed off. Ghost was in wedded bliss, and I didn't want to bother him with my issues. I reached over and grabbed my phone, and dialed Liberty's number from a blocked number.

"Hellooo," she sang into the phone. "Hello? Okay. Whoever keeps calling and not saying nothing, record my voice, it'll last longer," she snapped and ended the call.

I would sit and call her phone twice a day just to hear her voice. She sounded so different. A good different. Nonetheless, still different. Each time I called, I wanted to speak. I wanted to tell her that I missed her and that I was sorry for the shit I did. I didn't even need an apology from her, just her. That was all I needed and wanted from her. The Ring app on my phone went off and then the keys in the lock followed.

"Shaliq, where the hell are you? I know you saw me calling

you, boy," I heard my mother's voice. I was relieved that it wasn't Chanel's ass popping up.

"Ma, I haven't been in the mood. What do you need?"

She popped me in the head and then came around the couch. "I don't care if you haven't been in the mood, if I call you better come running."

"You're right, I'm sorry," I apologized and sat up. "What's going on?"

She tossed a paper at my head and stared at me. "Open it," she directed. "Never mind, never mind... Satin isn't your baby, Shaliq," she blurted.

"What? The hell you talking about?" I asked as I quickly opened the letter, she had tossed at me. I scanned the paper and what my mother had just blurted was true. "Where did you get this from?"

"When you left her with me to watch her I did a home DNA test."

"How? You didn't take DNA from me."

"Why do you think I made you brush your teeth? I knew it was something about that baby. Chanel never wanted her to come over and I couldn't connect with her. I connect with all my grandbabies. That damn baby looks too much like Chanel and nothing like you," she continued to vent, while I was trying to get my shit together.

How the fuck was this true? How could Chanel make me believe that this baby was mine and it wasn't? Chanel was my best friend, she wouldn't do no shit like that to me, would she? It was a question that I continued to ask and wonder while my mother sat there staring at me.

"Ma, this not right."

"You can choose not to believe a lot of things, but DNA doesn't lie. Satin isn't your daughter. I'm sorry it had to come from me, but I knew something wasn't right," she continued with her conspiracy. "And I know you like Maliah, but you need to get her checked too. These women be lying and wanting money, not baby daddies and that's exactly what Chanel did to you. Damn shame, y'all been friends for years."

"That's why I know she wouldn't do that shit to me." At this point, I think I was more delusional about the situation than anything. Chanel wouldn't do me like this, nah she couldn't do me like this. Even with all the shit we had going on, I knew she could never do me like this.

"Baby boy, I know Chanel is the only woman that has stuck around all these years. She's been your voice of reason and the person you have spent most of your time with, so I know it's hard to believe she would keep something like this from you, but you have the proof in your hands. Be honest, deep down you probably didn't feel like Satin was yours."

My mother knew me the best. For a while I questioned of Satin was mine. I mean, shit, she didn't have anything of me inside her. I waited because a baby's features changed a bunch of times, but even then, she looked more and more like Chanel and her side of the family. Nothing from me popped up. I even checked her ass cheek to see if she had the same birth mark I had, and she didn't. Even with all the doubt, I pushed it to the side and figured that she just looked like her mother and her genes were strong.

"What the fuck am I supposed to do with this information? I done built a bond with this baby, the hell I'm supposed to do, walk away?"

"She's young. She won't remember you. It will hurt for a while and I know it will. You have to do what's best for you, and raising someone else's child isn't it. You'll always resent Chanel for lying and putting you through this."

"She fucking made me lose the love of my life for it to not even be my damn baby!" I barked.

Chanel was the main reason why Liberty decided to end our relationship. I went to bat for Chanel's stupid ass instead of standing on my girl's side. I can feel how Liberty felt. She felt like Chanel would always come first, and it didn't matter what she could say, I would always be on the side of Chanel because she had my daughter. I did all of that to turn around and Satin not even be mine.

"You need to sit down and talk to her and hear her side."

"Nah, I need to beat the shit out of her with a damn Chanel belt," I said through gritted teeth.

"No, no, no. You need to sit and talk to her. Don't hurt that woman, she has a baby to raise at the end of the day." My mother warned. "I don't care how angry you are, Shaliq," she gave me a final warning and hugged me. "I'm sorry, baby. I'm so sorry."

"It's not your fault."

"I know, but I hate to see you hurting. I know you're hurting because of Liberty and then I had to bring you this bad news."

"It's all good. I'm gonna handle it," I smirked.

"I don't like that you're hurting. If you and Lib are meant to be, then you will be. I got an invitation to her wedding. I didn't even know she was getting married."

"She really going through with this?" I asked more to myself than my mother. "You going?"

"I am. You want to be my plus one?"

"Nah."

"You sure?"

"I'm good, mama. I promise. I need to handle one situation at a time."

"Okay. I can tell you're getting in that mood that means you don't want to be bothered. I'll call you later to check on you."

"Okay," I replied and sat seated on the couch thinking about all that was dropped into my lap. The devil was creating a web of mess that I had to fix. I wanted to kill Chanel so bad. My mom made me promise so I knew I couldn't.

Wanna go and get dinner tonight? I sent Chanel a text

message. It was the afternoon, so I had time to pull myself together and work on my facial expressions.

Sure. I been at work all day, so I'll go home and get Satin together. Want me to meet you?

Yeah. Applebee's.

Applebee's? What in the cheap.

I want their chicken pasta.

I'll make reservations at Bocelli's, she replied. *Their chicken pasta is ten times better.*

It always had to be expensive with her. She could never just sit and have a cheap meal. That was the thing I loved the most about Liberty. We could eat at McDonalds and she would never complain.

Ight. I replied

Chanel had me fucked up and hurt. As much as I complained that Satin didn't look like me, I loved that little girl. She was my heart and was supposed to be my first child. Even if she didn't know who the father was, she should have told me there could have been a possibility that I wasn't the father. I don't even know why she was fucking niggas while we were trying to get her pregnant. All this shit was too much for me to try and put together. I was trying hard not to let the beast out and do something to Chanel. The only thing that caused me to stop was the fact that despite how I felt, Satin needed her mother. Any other man probably would have been able to continue to raise a child that wasn't theirs, but I wasn't there. The hurt was there, and I would always want to reach across a table and choke Chanel whenever we got around each other. I couldn't front like this shit didn't hurt. Chanel wasn't just some random bitch. She was my best friend. We shared so much shit together and she knew shit about me that nobody knew.

After my shower, I quickly dressed and headed out. Chanel had sent me a text letting me know our reservation time. I was twenty minutes late, and she was texting me and telling me how I was rude and insensitive for inviting her and then having the nerve to be late. The nerve of her to fucking tell me how I was insensitive and rude. I continued to the restaurant and pulled up ten minutes later. The valet took my car and I strolled in. I didn't even need the hostess to seat me because I saw Chanel sitting at the table cooing at Satin. In a perfect world, this would be my small family. Chanel wouldn't have turned out to be some bitch I couldn't stand, and Satin would be my daughter.

"About damn time," she scoffed when she saw me. "How you invite me out to eat and then show up late," she continued to complain.

"I didn't pick this place, you did."

"All I'm saying is that you had me and your daughter waiting," she made sure to add. "Enough about that, I ordered our food already."

"K."

"Why are you being so short with me? What is going on with you? You're not shaven and you look like you didn't even try to get dressed," she picked apart my appearance.

I shrugged and grabbed the water. "I told you I wanted to go to Applebee's. You don't have to get dressed up to go to Applebee's."

"Whatever. So, I've been going around with the realtor and I think I found the perfect townhouse in a great neighborhood. Oh, and I need a new car, maybe a jeep for the baby," she ran down the list of demands that she needed for herself, more than the baby.

"Your car is good. You have one baby, not six."

"Well, Priest bought Justice a Rolls Royce truck," she mentioned. I knew it would make it back to her soon. Justice was the only one riding around here with that truck. Shit, I wasn't even riding around like that yet. My ass was still on the waiting list. Me and Priest both got put on the list the same time. That nigga shelled out some money to get his before mine.

"How you know her business?" I played it off.

"Stop trying to play me. Everybody is talking about her driving around with that car. She gets her hair done by one of my close friends and she was on the phone getting new furniture for a condo he had bought her in the Yacht Club gated community too."

I knew about all of this because Priest had asked me what I thought about that community. It was a nice one and had the security I knew he wanted for Justice since she refused to move in with him. The only downside was that the shit was expensive to get in there and the HOA fees were outrageous. Priest was cool blowing money like that, but I wasn't the same. Especially when Chanel's ass was always doing everything to let everyone know that she had a nigga that would drop money on her.

"Why you worried about her? Whatever Priest and Justice got going on is their business," I told her. From her face, I could tell that she didn't like what I said.

"She popped his baby out and look what she's getting. Free is living in that huge mansion in Jersey and drives all those foreign cars."

"Chanel, why the fuck is any of this your business? What does any of that have to do with us?"

"Because I'm tired of just being your baby mama that is fucking struggling. I've been down before any of those bitches and look at how they're living."

"You serious right now?"

"Dead serious."

"You got some fucking nerve to use struggling in any sentence when it comes to me. That baby shower was fifty-thousand-dollars. Did I complain once? Nah, I let you do your thing. Everything that Satin has needed, I paid for, including paying half of your insurance fee when you had her. Tell me what have you been struggling with? She's never been out of diapers because I have six boxes dropped off every week along with formula. You were even able to extend your maternity leave longer because I made sure you had bread in your pocket."

She folded her arms. "You do all that to keep me quiet. I planned that baby shower with my mom and you offered no input, but with money. You do your part as a father, and you're complaining?"

My blood was boiling because she was pissing me off with the selfish shit she was saying. How the fuck was she complaining because I wouldn't pay for a new place or car? She drove a new enough car and as far as her old apartment, she fought me when it came to moving in the first place. Now, she wanted to get a new apartment because she saw what Priest and Ghost was doing for Justice and Free. Never mind the fact that Justice and Free knew who the fuck their baby father was.

"Bitch, Satin isn't even my fucking baby!" I yelled and tossed the paper at her. It slapped her lip before falling onto the table.

"W...what are you talking about?" she stammered.

"My mom did a DNA test and it turns out that I'm not Satin's fucking father."

"This isn't real. Satin is your daughter, why would I lie about that?"

I closed my eyes and rubbed my temples because I could tell she was lying. It had been something I had become good at because we were so close. "Lie to me again. Fucking lie to me again," I threatened.

She put the paper down and sighed. "I had slept with Fat Tony one night after a party. It was a mistake and I regretted it, we never had sex again. When I got pregnant, I thought it was your baby and didn't question it."

"Fuck you, Chanel. You fucking ruined my relationship

with Liberty and my dumb ass continued to fucking take your side when she tried to put me onto game about you."

"Fuck Liberty's crack head ass. You shouldn't be listening to anyone who gets fucking high. Period. You let that bitch come around and try to change our dynamic. We were good before she came into the fucking picture."

"Nah, you thought we were good. I let you use and manipulate me from jump. Anytime that you needed something, I was there for you. When it came for you to be there for me, you were never around. I sacrificed and did more for you in our friendship than you did for me."

"Bullshit. I've been there for you more times that I can count. You let bitches get in your mind and cloud what the fuck we had."

"Nah, I let you get in my mind and cloud my judgement. Then, you fucking lie about Satin being mine."

"I didn't know that she wasn't yours. I swear."

"When everybody was telling me how much of a thot you were and how you be fucking everybody in the hood, I didn't believe them because I knew you. Look at me being the fool because you been fucking everybody and I was looking like the damn sucka ass nigga."

Tears fell down her face as she looked at me. "She's your daughter. You've been there since day one, Shaliq."

"Nah, she's your daughter. How the fuck you expect me to sit and raise Fat Tony's daughter? You better go tell that fat nigga that he got a baby. I hope you let his wife know too," I got up from the table.

Chanel grabbed my hand and looked into my eyes. "Shaliq, please... we need you."

Seeing her crying and hurt would have worked back in the day, but not anymore. Chanel did something that I couldn't forgive. It wasn't even about all the money I had spent. It was the principal. If my mother didn't do the test, what would have happened? I would have been raising another man's baby. That shit was fucked up.

"Nah, when you had me you acted like I wasn't doing enough. I'm good, Chanel. Enjoy motherhood though," I removed my hand and left her at the table. She let out a loud sob when I made it to the door.

I don't know what the future held. If me and Chanel could repair our friendship, but I knew one thing, I wanted to get my girl back – Asap.

CHANEL HAD CALLED me almost every day since last week. I ignored her and turned my phone off because she continued to keep calling me. Her mother even tried to reach out to me about the situation. I guess she realized her daughter's golden ticket had died. Chanel did some shit that I couldn't forgive or act like didn't happen. I mean, I was there for Satin through everything. The doctor appointments when she was still in Chanel's stomach, her birth and I even cut her umbilical cord. Shit, I signed her birth certificate too. I had my lawyer finding out a way to remove myself from the birth certificate so I wouldn't have any financial ties to Chanel and Satin. It hurt like hell to walk away from that little girl because she didn't deserve that shit. It wasn't her fault that her mother wanted to spread her fucking legs and end up pregnant with her. Chanel was crying and sad for her, not because of Satin. Fat Tony would never accept that baby out loud. He would give Chanel hush money and have her living lavish, but behind his wife's back.

"You gonna come in or sit out there for another hour?" Maliah came out the house. She had on a tight short romper. You could see her protruding belly. She was all stomach. This was one person I didn't have to question when it came to my son. I knew I was his father and that Maliah would never do me like that.

"I was thinking. Hold your horses," I laughed and got out the car. Maliah had been trying to get me over here since last week. She said she had to talk to me about something important.

"Yeah, whatever... it's like pulling teeth to get you over here," she rubbed her stomach and held the door open for me.

I stopped in the doorway and rubbed her stomach. It wasn't huge, but it was big enough to hold and rub. "Damn, he growing in there, huh?"

"Yeah. The doctor says everything looks good."

"Good. Good," I walked into her house as she shut the door behind me.

She walked into the kitchen and grabbed me some water. "I'm so excited for him to come. Me and Mariah are going to start the nursery soon."

"Do I get a say?"

"If you want," she messed with the loose strand of hair hanging in her face. "I didn't think you cared about that stuff."

"On the real, I want to be a part of everything with you and my son. I'm gonna start coming to appointments, just let me know when they are. I don't want you to feel like you're going through this alone. You don't complain and handle shit and I think I got used to that. I should be at every appointment."

"I appreciate that. I know you have a lot going on, so I try to not bother you when it comes to stuff like that."

"Anything that has to do with you and my son, I care about."

She smiled. "My mom went to my last appointment."

My eyes widened. I didn't expect her to ever go to an appointment. "Word? How did that go?"

"She heard from my dad when my next appointment was, so she was in the waiting room when I arrived. She still rolls her eyes at the fact that we're having a baby together, but I think she's excited for the baby."

"And what about y'all relationship?"

"We had lunch at the house, and we spoke about a lot. My mom revealed a lot to me and I think we connected on something more than just the streets. I'm happy, for real."

"I'm happy for you. It's important that our son is born into love."

"Yes, very important. I want to have the baby at my parent's house. A natural birth."

I put my hands to my face. "You would want to do some shit like this, right?"

She giggled. "I did my research and I want to be in a comfortable place with family around. Would you get into the pool too?"

"You gonna be shitting and blood in there... for you, I'll put a wet suit and get in there."

"Deal," she held out her hand and we shook on it. "I do need to talk to you about something," her face changed. I could tell whatever she was about to say was going to be important.

"Oh God... what's up?"

"I know you still love Liberty. Even with you both not being together, I know that you love her and that love won't fade away anytime soon," she started.

"I'm not going to front; I do still love her. It's something that I have to work on and get under control," I admitted.

"You shouldn't have to get your feelings under control. If you love her, then you should be able to be with her."

"Malia—"

"Listen to me. I'm tired of competing with her for a piece of your heart. I love you, and you know that," she wiped her tears that fell from her eyes. "I'm so damn emotional with this pregnancy." "I love you and will always be here for you, you know that too. I think it's best for us to go back to being friends and be the best damn parents to our son. As hard as it is for me to end whatever it is that we have, I know it's something we need to do for the both of us, and for the sake of our son."

I walked and sat down next to her on the couch. Wrapping my arms around her, I kissed her on the cheeks. "You know I love you too, right?"

"I do, which is why I know you need to do this. I saw first-hand how what you and Chanel had ruined your friendship once you had Satin," she sniffled. "I don't want that to be us. I want to continue to be the person you call to come chill with you in the trap. I still want to be able to come lay on your couch when I'm bored of being home. Our friendship means more to me than trying to force a relationship when I know your heart isn't into it," she leaned her head on my shoulder.

"I agree. You're my nigga for life, you already know that. If we need to stop fucking, then I guess."

Maliah giggled. "Staten!" she squealed. "I think we need to focus on our son and welcoming him into the world. I'm building my relationship back with my mom, shit is looking up for us."

I wasn't ready to tell Maliah about me and Chanel yet. It was too fresh and new for me to want to speak about it. In due time, I knew I would be laying across her couch and spilling my problems like she was my therapist.

"Shit is def looking up," I rubbed her stomach as we laid back on the couch. Maliah could always sense shit and I knew she was picking up my actions. I was barely around and when I did come around, I was distracted.

"Feel," she moved my hand to her stomach. "You hear daddy?" she spoke to her stomach and I smiled hella big.

"Yeah, he's the most important," I continued to rub her stomach. Nothing in this world mattered as much as this moment.

15

Liberty

"What do you think about the dress?" I asked Free, as she pecked away at her phone. She was on a lunch break and had decided to pop in at my fitting. I had picked out my dress with Ty's mother and I fell in love with it. Neither of my sisters had seen the dress and I wanted them to see it. Justice said she had things to do and Free was at work but made time to pop her head in and see the dress.

"I like it," she said with her head still in her phone.

"And the fur around the neckline isn't too much?" I pondered.

"Nope, it adds the perfect touch."

"Damn lie. I don't have no fur on this damn dress," I called her out.

She looked up from her phone and decided to slip it into her purse. "Sorry, this new client I have has been on my staff's nerves and they sent her to me to deal with. I like the dress."

"Damn, Free. You can act like you're excited for me. I was excited for you and Ghost when he told me."

"Well, we been together and knew each other longer than you and Ty. I know nothing about this man and you're about to marry him."

"You don't need to know anything about him. I'm the one marrying him," I snapped.

None of my sisters were excited for me to get married. Planning a wedding was supposed to be the best thing in the world for some brides. You had your family to help you plan your special day. Your sisters usually told you they hated a million dresses before they told you they liked that one special dress. I had none of that and felt so alone in this. It wasn't only my sisters either, it was Ty as well. He was always working and gone. I think I had seen him twice in this entire month. When he wasn't around, he sent his mother to help me with stuff.

"So, stop expecting me to be happy for you. I'm not," she admitted what I already knew. "You've been out the rehab for what, a month already and you're planning a wedding. What about working on yourself?"

"Do I get into you and Justice's business? I'm always there to talk and listen to you guys, but when it comes to me, you both feel like you're my mother and need to tell me what to do with my life."

She stood up. "If you want to marry him, then do it. Liberty, you know you're still in love with Staten and you're trying to use Ty as a cover-up."

"Why would I still love him? With all that he put me through."

Freedom laughed. "Put you through," she continued to laugh. "All that man did was try and love your stubborn ass. He lost a piece of himself becoming so wrapped into you."

"Yeah, he was so wrapped into me that he got Maliah pregnant."

"And you're about to get married, so you're both even. He and Maliah aren't even together. All he does is work and focus on himself, like you should be doing."

"How did you get to be so perfect?"

"What are you talking about?"

"Oh, I assumed that you were perfect from the way you're telling me shit that I need to do. You're not perfect and just because you're married, doesn't mean your relationship is perfect either."

Free rolled her eyes. "We're not perfect. I never said we were. Lib, you're going to do what you want, despite what I say. If you think that marrying Ty is going to change your life, then do it. Has he even met Chance?"

"No, he's been busy with work."

"That man is too busy to meet the most important part of your life. Hmph, maybe that should tell you something," she put her purse over her shoulders and headed toward the door. "Call you later, I have to get back to work," she said before leaving.

I stood there in my wedding dress feeling so sad. This was supposed to be the best moment of my life and it felt like I was doing something wrong. "We can take it out slightly. You've gained some weight since last time," the seamstress said as she pinned things.

Since Ty convinced me to quit my job, all I did was binge watch TV, eat and plan this wedding. I didn't work out or do anything because I would be so comfortable in the bed. It didn't help that he had a housekeeper that tended to the house. The weight looked good on me, so I wasn't complaining. Between doing coke, stressing and not taking care of myself the right way, I had lost a lot of weight and was starting to see it in my face.

"Okay," I replied and went to the back to take the dress off. While I sat in the dressing room, I decided to call Ty.

He'd always been able to lift my spirits when I was feeling down.

"Hey babe, what you doing?" he answered with the screen black.

"Better if I could see you," I giggled.

His face came onto the screen. "Sorry about that. I'm at the hotel trying to get some sleep before someone come and knock on my door."

"Well, I just wanted to see your face and speak to you. I miss you, when are you coming home?"

"I was supposed to come home tomorrow, but I'm gonna stay a few extra days to make sure everything is running smoothly."

"Our cake tasting is this week, you're gonna miss that too?"

"You know I don't care about that stuff. All I care about is marrying you. Pick something good."

I sighed.

"Why you giving me that face?"

"I'm tired of being alone all the time. I mean, I like my alone time, but you haven't been home at all."

"I know and I'm trying to scale back the hours."

"This is scaling back the hours?" I blurted. "I don't think you're going to be around for our wedding."

He laughed. "I'm gonna be home, push the cake tasting and I'll be there... promise."

"K."

"What are your plans for the day?"

"Home. You know I don't have a life."

"I was thinking you should throw a bridal shower. My mom had mentioned something about it, and I think it will be something good and positive for you."

"Me and my sisters aren't in the best place, and people usually throw that for the bride, not the bride."

"I'll have my mom throw you one," he suggested.

"I'm really not in the mood for that, babe. I appreciate you wanting to do that for me, but I think I would rather have a date night with you in the same city."

"Oh, you think you're funny."

"Yeah, a little bit."

"Look, I want you to have your special day, so if I have to throw you one, I will."

"Okay," I smiled. Ty was super sweet like that. All he wanted was for me to smile. I got irritated with him because he worked so damn much. I had to make an appointment just to see my man.

"Talk to you later. Call me when you take your bubble bath later."

"Will do," I ended the call.

I got dressed and signed some papers and left to head home. Ty moved everything out of my apartment. I tried to convince him to allow me to have my own place and he wasn't having it. He told me that my apartment had too many bad memories and I had to agree. We moved all my stuff except clothes into storage and I had been living in his condo. It was a high rise and had beautiful views of the city. How could I complain when I didn't have to work and got to live like this?

I kicked my shoes off in the foyer and went straight to the fridge to grab some juice. After popping the top into the sink, I took a gulp and leaned against the counter with my head back. I hated arguing with my sisters. It was something we always did since we were younger and always made up. It seemed like the older we got, the longer it took for us to make-up with each other. Justice wasn't back to speaking to me fully. Whenever she was around, she would say a few words, nothing more. I knew not to push her, so I accepted whatever conversation she did get me. Me and Free seemed to be the only two on the same page, well, except for today. Whenever I mentioned the wedding, I noticed her attitude and ignored it. Today, she was so loud with the attitude and feelings that I had no choice but to address. I tried ignoring it because I knew she didn't want this for me, but today it was something that I couldn't ignore anymore. Free did what she wanted and didn't give a damn what anyone had to say. Why couldn't I do the same? Why couldn't I live my life and make no apologies?

"I didn't realize you came in," Kat, the housekeeper came out the master bedroom.

"I thought you would have been gone for the day."

"Ty called and told me to run you a bubble bath. He said that you needed it," I smiled because I knew he would do something like this.

"He always thinks a bubble bath is the key to everything," I smirked to myself. "Thank you, Kat. You can leave for the day, if you're done."

"I'm done. I'll see you tomorrow," she replied and gathered her things to leave for the day. I walked into the bathroom and saw she had run the bath and put rose petals all over the top of the bath water.

"Ty, you're too good to be true," I spoke to myself and undressed to sit in the bed.

As I eased into the tub, I couldn't help but to question if this was the life I wanted to live. Did I want to be a wife to a man that was never home? What Free said kept repeating in my head. Ty hadn't made time to meet Chance and it bothered me. I tried to act like it didn't, but it did. Chance was the most important part of my life and he couldn't make time just to visit him with me. Did that mean that other important dates in our life that I would have to spend alone? I liked my alone time, yet, if I was married, it didn't make sense to be alone all the time when I had a husband.

These were all things that I needed to take into consideration when it came to marrying Ty. I wasn't sure if I was cool with him being away all the time. When he did come back, it was like I had to get to know him all over again. It also didn't help the fact that I missed and thought about Staten all the time. Free had told me about Chanel and all I wanted to do was comfort him. I heard about Maliah through mutual friends and I wasn't surprised. I always suspected that Maliah had a little crush on him. What confused me was that they weren't together. I for sure thought that they would have been together. Hearing Free tell me that they weren't together. Maliah still conducted herself like regular, even while being pregnant. When she saw me, she still spoke and flashed a smile.

My heart was torn. I knew that I needed something new and Ty brought that to me. Then, Staten was familiar, and I knew the love was there. We had a lot of issues to pan out, yet the love kind of outweighed all of that. I knew at the end of the day that he would always be there when it was all said and done. He would lay down his life if that meant protecting me. With Ty, I didn't get that vibe. Especially since I spent more time with myself than with him. This wasn't like me. I didn't beg a nigga to be around him. It made me feel weird as hell. I finished my bath and then went to grab something to eat. I made a quick sandwich and then laid in the bed with my robe on chewing. I had everything at my fingertips, yet I was laying in this bed confused on what I should do. I closed my eyes and before I knew it, I was asleep.

"Thank you," they both said, and I went to the supplies closet to grab some of the things needed.

"Move Liberty!" I heard one of the doctors yelling as they pushed a hospital bed down the hall at full speed. At quick glance, I saw Staten in the bed unconscious.

"Staten?" I yelled.

"You know him?" one of the nurses asked. "He came in with a little girl. Their car was shot up," she informed me.

I gasped with tears in my eyes. We had just seen each other earlier and he said he had his nieces with him. "Where's the little girl?" I questioned. My hands were shaking, and I felt like I couldn't breathe.

"Down the hall to the right. I was just going there to check her vitals. She had four bullets removed from her. They decided to leave one inside because it would have been too risky to remove," she informed me as we walked the hall. It felt like we walked miles before we finally came to the room. The shades were down and, on that hall, where there was only one other room. "He was in this room. We haven't been able to contact any family yet. There's another little girl, but she's with social services right now."

"No, no, she has a family," I told her as we entered the room. I broke down seeing this little baby attached to so many machines. All you heard was beeping throughout the room. A machine was breathing for her. No one should be in this situation, but it hurt even more knowing it was a baby.

"If you're family, you can go down there and let them know. It's been all hands-on deck trying to keep them both stabled. Thankfully, she hasn't coded. The surgery was successful. The male, he was hit the worst. When they found him, he was shielding the girls in the back seat. His back was riddled with bullets and he had been hit in his left shoulder."

"Oh my God," I gasped as I sat down in the chair and tried to collect my thoughts. I quickly left the room and dialed Free's phone. She didn't answer so I tried again.

"Dang, what do you want?" she answered. "Mama is praying over Justice right now."

"Is Ghost with you?" I asked with a shaky voice. I was pacing the hallway because I couldn't believe this was happening. As a nurse I had to check my feelings at the door. Except, I knew these people.

"Yeah, he right here... Why?"

"Free, just put him on the phone, please," I begged.

"Lib, why do you sound like that?"

"Free, just put him on the fucking phone!" I screamed and he soon came on the line.

"Yo, what's good?"

"You need to come to Staten Island hospital. G, what I'm 'bout to tell you... you need to calm down, check your feelings and get here quick."

"Yo, you scaring me... what the fuck is up?"

"Staten and Summer have been shot!" I broke down crying. "The car was riddled with bullets and Staten has coded a bunch of times. He's being brought up to surgery again."

The line was quiet. "What?" he roared.

"CODE WHITE! CODE WHITE!" I heard over the loud speaker and looked back at the room. Code white meant it was a pediatric emergency. When I turned to the room, the doctor I was talking to had come out the room.

"Liberty pass me the pediatric crash cart!" she yelled to me.

"Ghost, your baby is coding," I sobbed as I stood there crippled with fear. Everything was happening so fast and slow at the same time. The sounds of people's voices sounded muffled as I stood there clutching my phone in my hand. I could hear Ghost screaming on the phone and my heart hurt for him.

I gasped as I jumped out of my sleep. Holding my heart, I looked out the floor to ceiling window and noticed that it was now dark outside. Looking on the clock on the table, it was ten at night. My heart was still beating rapidly as I thought about the day Summer died and Staten had almost lost his life too. With my hands shaking, I sent Free a text message.

Can you send me Staten's new number? I texted her. Free had been working day and night on her work projects, so I knew that she would reply back. Just like I expected, she replied with his contact bubble in our text message thread.

Thanks.

She never replied and it was probably because she was still in her feelings about our argument earlier. I dialed his number and leaned up in the bed with my hand rested on my heart. It wouldn't calm down until I heard his voice.

"Yo, who this?" his groggy voice answered on the other line.

"It's Liberty. Hey," I replied, feeling better that I had heard his voice.

I could hear him sitting up from wherever he was laying. "What's good? You alright?"

"Yes, I'm fine. I had a dream about the night you crashed when I was working. Just wanted to make sure that you were alright."

"Yeah, I'm good. Just fell asleep reading over a contract."

"Contract?"

"Yeah. I bought a barbershop and want to make sure everything good with it."

"Cool. I'm happy for you."

"I'm happy fo—"

"Do you still love me?" I cut him off. I had to know if he still loved me the way I loved him. Yes, it was easier to hide it because I hated how he treated me, but I still loved this man and couldn't act like I didn't. Free had called me out at a lunch with Justice and I denied, even though I knew my sister knew what I was feeling. It was bad that I was lying in another man's condo, wanting to be laid up in Staten's arms.

"I think you know the answer to that already."

"I want to hear you say it," I needed to hear him tell me. I had to hear his voice when he said it.

"I still love you; Liberty and I have never stopped loving you," he admitted.

I put the phone to my chest and leaned back in the bed with my eyes closed. "Babe? You sleep already?" I heard Ty's voice.

"I'll call you back," I told Staten.

"Nah. Be happy, Lib. Take care," he told me and ended the call.

Ty came into the bedroom with roses and a Louis Vuitton

gift bag. I offered him a weak smile. "I thought you were staying longer?"

"I heard your voice and figured that I would come home and surprise you. I know it's hard with me working all the time and I never want my future wife to feel neglected."

I had the perfect man standing in front of me, but all that was running through my mind was Shaliq Davis. He was who I wanted, and it was sad that a dream about him getting shot made me realize that.

"I appreciate that."

"I have to fly out tomorrow morning to Milan for a few weeks. I'll be back a day before the wedding," he made sure to tell me.

"Okay," I replied.

"I'm gonna go shower. Stay in that robe because I missed exploring that body," he told me and loosened his tie on his way to the bathroom. I laid back and waited for my future husband to come back from the shower.

PRINCETON, New Jersey
    The Davis' Residence

TY HAD BEEN in Milan for a week and was apparently living his best life. I was in meeting after meeting regarding the wedding. I was the one who had to deal with his mother wanting to pick things out. Ty was a mama's boy and the more I was around his mother and him, I figured that out. He didn't make moves unless his mother was involved in it. While I thought that him proposing to me was random and living on the edge, turns out that he spoke to his mother before doing it. She let that slip out when we were cake tasting. Ty did all that popping up to surprise me just to fly off and miss the cake tasting. I was tired of being alone and feeling like I was planning a wedding for me and his mother. Don't get me wrong, she was a sweet woman and I would be lucky to have her as a mother in law. The fact remained that I had built a better relationship with her than her son.

When I woke up this morning, I had roses waiting on the kitchen counter with a sweet letter from Ty. He had Kat run down the street to the flower stand and get it for me. He also had her sign the card. Then, he had breakfast sent upstairs to me to enjoy before booking me some time at the spa, then the hair salon. All of that was nice and appreciated. After I ate breakfast, I went into my closet to find something to wear and sobbed. I sobbed so hard that Kat knocked on the door a few times to get me to answer. I felt empty. Some women would kill for a man like Ty. A man that took care of his woman and didn't have a problem with doing it. Me, I was different. I liked alone time, but I also wanted to feel like I was in a relationship too. I wanted to feel like I was a priority in your life, and with Ty I didn't feel that. Waking up to flowers, breakfast and a day booked at the spa wasn't the life that I wanted to live. It wasn't who I was. I wanted to wake up in bed and have sex, crack jokes and then roll out the bed and go grab some breakfast from Denny's.

I sent Kat home early, packed up my bags and had the door man help me load it up into my truck. I took all my clothes and things that I needed, then left Ty a note on the counter. I doubted that he would ever find the note since he was barely home. I'm sure Kat would find it and call him tomorrow. I drove all the way to Free's house and now I was sitting outside after being let into the gate an hour ago. Gathering the courage to crawl back to my sister who told me that I wasn't happy was hard. Free called everything that I was feeling. She knew me and knew that I would never be happy living the life that Ty provided. I loved to work and quitting my job was probably one of the hardest things that I had to do.

I didn't even notice there were a bunch of cars everywhere. Ghost had a lot of cars, but not this damn many. Blue balloons littered the entrance to the house and that's when I remembered that today was Maliah's baby shower. Free had told me that Ghost volunteered to throw it for Staten, since everything happened with Chanel. I think he wanted to throw it more because he was not pleased at Chanel's baby shower. I walked slowly into the house and declined the drink that was offered soon as I walked in. Everyone seemed to be enjoying everything. I slipped throughout the party looking for my sister. I spotted Maliah walking upstairs and followed her up there.

"Liberty, Jesus, you scared the shit out of me," she held her stomach and chest at the same time. "What are you doing here?"

"I broke my engagement and have nowhere to live, so I came to talk to my sister. I had forgot your shower was today."

"Broke your engagement, huh?"

"Yes, why you say it like that?"

"You want Staten back."

"Are you asking me or telling me?"

"I'm telling you. I know that the both of you crave each other. He doesn't speak much on you, but I know he wants you more than anything, and I know you want him too."

"Don't you have a little crush on him?"

"Don't do that, Liberty. I'm a grown woman carrying his baby. I know that you have his heart and no matter how cool, beautiful and how bomb sex is between us, I would never have his heart the way that you do."

"I'm sorry."

"You're fine. All I ask is that you respect me as his baby mother and love my son too. Me and Staten will remain friends while co-parenting our son."

"I can respect that."

"Go and get your man," she smirked. "I have to pee so bad."

"Where is he?"

"Should be downstairs in the theater room. The baby shower thing isn't his thing, so he was watching Creed down there."

I jetted down the stairs and bumped into Free. She asked me something, but I was on a mission. She called behind me as I found the steps that led downstairs and took them two at a time. I was quiet when I entered the theater. He was laid out in the middle chair with his hat pulled low over his eyes. I just knew he was asleep because he could never stay awake during a movie.

"The fuck you standing over me for, Liberty?" I damn near jumped out my skin. Hell, I thought he was fast asleep.

"I thought you were sleep."

"I was, but you breathing all fucking hard woke me up... What's up?" he leaned up and removed his hat.

"I don't know how to say thi—"

"Don't start spilling your feelings like you did when you got out of rehab the first time. I don't have time to deal with us getting back together, then you feeling a way and ending this. I'm tired of getting my heart broke, so if that's what you on, go ahead and go back to your fiancé."

"I ended it with him. I wasn't sure of anything in my entire life, but you, you make me feel so secure and sure of us. I push away because knowing how much I love you scares me. It's easier to push you away and hide my feelings for you than to confront them head on," I stopped and sat in the chair beside him. "I love you and I have never stopped loving you."

"You're the most complicated, hard headed and weird ass person I have ever met," he said and I dropped my head. "But, I think that's the reason I love you. The way we vibe when we're good is the reason I held out to hope that you would come back to me."

"I'm selfish, mean, distant and I'm a recovering drug addict. That's enough to make any nigga go running, yet you always run toward me and choose me. I want to make this work. I want us to do this and grow from it."

"Lib, as much as I love you, I don't want to jump into this with you again," I put my head down, and he used his index finger to lift my head up. "Unless you're all in with me. You gotta let me in. When you hide shit, I get suspicious and that's when I act like your sober coach. I want to love you, not raise you or feel like I'm your father... feel me?"

I nodded my head because I understood what he said. "I'm not perfect, but I promise that I'll do better. I promise."

"And I'll promise that I won't be so hard on you. I'll support, love and protect you with my heart, Liberty."

I climbed into the chair into his lap and he wrapped his arms around me. "I love you so much, Staten. I do."

"I love you too," he kissed me on the forehead as we sat in the theater just taking in each other's presence.

EPILOGUE

Six Months Later...
Justice

"Baby, look at the camera, look... okay, stand there... right there, right there, Gyson!" Free yelled as she directed him as she recorded a video.

"Yo, ring that muthafucka to the bell drop on the floor. We'll replace it!" Staten yelled, as we stood there waiting for Ghost to ring the remission bell. Everyone was here waiting to see what we all had been praying for.

Ghost had taken his last round of chemo and was officially in remission. We all had tears in our eyes, but Staten had tears coming down his face as he cried and hung his arm around his brother. "Go uncle!" Kiki yelled as she clapped her hands.

"Fuck that bitch ass cancer, thought he was going to take my brother, fuck that shit!" he sniffled.

"I wanna thank you all for being there for me during this time. I know I couldn't be the best brother, uncle, son or even husband because I was always sick, but y'all held it down for me and that's what family is about. I'm happy to have all of you in my life and appreciate every one of you," he said as he held onto the rope. "This is for you, Summer!" he looked up and rang the bell hard as fuck.

Tears came down my eyes because we had prayed so hard for Ghost to beat this. These past few months had been hard as hell on all of us. Especially for Ghost and Free. Even with everything going on, he made sure he was there for everyone as much as he could. I loved how he loved my sister, and I loved how my sister loved him too. They weren't perfect, lord knows they weren't, still they were still worth it. I hugged Ghost as Free continued to record pictures.

Me and Priest were still not together, but we were working on it. He was working hard as hell, as he should have. Priest wanted his family bad and I could tell from how hard he worked. I moved into the condo he bought me because whether I agreed with him or not, me and Yasmine needed to be safe. Priest didn't spend the night or any of that. He came over to spend time with Yasmine if she wasn't over his house. My education center opened, and all my time was spent there. It felt so good to teach again. I had been so occupied with other shit that I lost focus on my true love and that was teaching. I went to work every morning excited to help kids that needed it. Every day we had new parents signing their children up to come to our center. Even though I was single; I wasn't looking or dating. I needed to fall in love with me again. Priest was still the love of my life and I was sure we would make it work down the line. Right now, I was focused on me and he understood that. Even though he didn't spend the night, I did help myself to riding his dick after Yasmine went to bed. When Priest told me that he would never hurt me like that again, I believed him. Just because I believed he wouldn't, didn't mean that he still didn't have to earn me back. All I could say, was pray for us. I was ready for baby two but wanted to wait until we were more stable before welcoming another baby into the mix.

Lavern got back with her husband and made sure to send Priest a post card from Aruba. I was convinced that bitch was nuts. As much as Priest said she understood when they spoke, I don't think it hit her. The only reason she got back with her husband was because she couldn't have Priest. The phone calls did stop, and I was glad for that. She had been on my nerves with the damn phone calls and I was happy that Priest was able to get her to stop. Our daughter was so beautiful, healthy and sassy. She was the apple of our eyes and made me stop and thank God for such a precious gift. Her cute self was the reason I wanted a little brother or sister for her. Me and Priest made cute kids. Kiki ended up moving in with me. With Love running around loose and out of control, and Kiss trying to move in with Mirror, I needed to keep an eye on her. I home-schooled her at the center every day, and I had her back into dance along with therapy. Priest was happy that she moved with me because he just knew he was going to be next. And, boy was he wrong. If he wanted to move in together, I needed a commitment and a big ass house to match.

Staten and Liberty were back together, and everyone was happy. Liberty was still clean. Liberty didn't have anywhere to stay, so she was living with Free. Staten didn't want to jump into living with each other right away, which I thought was smart. They didn't need to be living together. Both of them were in couple's therapy so they could learn how to deal with each other. Staten needed to learn how to be Liberty's man and not her guardian, and Liberty had to learn how to be more opened and receptive to love when it was shown to her. Liberty eventually called Ty, and they were able to laugh about them getting married so soon. He wasn't ready to be married and realized he loved being single and traveling the world. He even let her keep the ring and Staten took the shit and tossed it over a bridge when they drove to Brooklyn from Staten island. He replaced the ring with a promise ring. He told her he promised to love, protect and always honor her.

Maliah had Shaolin Vero Davis. He was so handsome and this time he looked just like Staten. It was so weird how he had his same expressions and everything. You couldn't tell Staten nothing about his son. Maliah, Liberty and Staten all had a good relationship. Liberty even picked Shaolin up when Maliah had to handle business. They all got along because they both knew their position. Maliah dropped that baby like it was nothing and got back to work. If possible, she was putting in more work than before she was pregnant. Messiah and Staten were back on speaking terms. As much as she hated their situation, she couldn't ignore the fact that Staten was a good father and that he loved and cared for Maliah as his baby mother. As for Chanel, she got her wish... kinda.

She finally told Fat Tony that he was the father of Satin. He got a test and sure enough he was the father. He moved her out of her parent's house into a townhouse she wanted, and then got her new jeep. She was rolling around in the same G wagon that Free was. The downside was that she was always second and so was Satin. Oh, and she had to fuck his fat greasy ass whenever he did come to visit her and their daughter. My hair-stylist spilled all the tea on how Chanel hated being Fat Tony's kept woman and that she didn't want to fuck with him anymore but had nowhere to go. The dumb bunny quit her damn job, so she had to depend on his big ass. Staten hadn't spoke to her since he left the restaurant. If it wasn't about his son, Liberty or Maliah, he didn't give a damn. Those three had built what Chanel couldn't have had with Liberty. They actually co-existed and were able to have a healthy relationship with each other. It wasn't for everybody, but it worked for them.

Free and Ghost were planning baby number five sometime this year. Rain really wanted a baby sister, so they were going to try for a baby girl. Samoor's heart condition was still something they battled, but baby boy was good. We would always worry about him because his heart condition was important. I was glad that some stress could finally come off of Free. She worried about Samoor and then Ghost. Now, she could focus strictly on Samoor and not stress herself out anymore. Our mama decided to sell her house and travel all over the world. It wasn't a surprise because we knew she wasn't happy just being a grandmother. Mama Rae had stepped in and became like a second mother for me. That woman didn't know how much I appreciated her. As far as me and Liberty's relationship, we were trying. That was all I could say. Not a day went by that I didn't think about how I found her. We spoke more which was good. I saw her trying and I was proud of her. She volunteered down at the educa-tion center a few times a week. Staten told her she could go back to work, or she could work with him at the barbershop, and she chose to help him run the barbershop. I loved how patient and loving he was with her. It never changed, no matter how pissed she made him.

Everyone was living their lives and we were all happy. Life isn't about happy endings, and although some of our situations aren't the way we had envisioned, I can say we were all happy. I was able to have a beautiful baby girl, and work on my relation-ship with her father. Ghost beat cancer and was able to live another day to be with all them damn kids they had. Liberty was trying to be a better person and focusing on her sobriety. Free's company was booming like it always has been. I could see she was happy because she smiled more. Designing was her first love and she had fell back into love with it. I loved my family. We had been through so much, so being able to take a breath felt good as hell.

"Lib, stop rubbing your ass on my dick. You making me hard," Staten felt the need to announce in the room.

"You're nasty, I'm trying to squeeze into the damn picture. Perv," she snapped back and we all started to laugh.

The End

Make sure to follow me on social media!
www.facebook.com/JahquelJ
http://www.instagram.com/_Jahquel
http://www.twitter.com/Author_Jahquel
Be sure to join my reader's group on Facebook
www.facebook.com/ Jahquel's we reading or nah?

PLEASE MAKE SURE YOU ANSWER THE QUESTIONS SO YOU CAN BE ACCEPTED!

Coming 06/24!